YOUR BODY IS A FEVER DREAM

A New Weird Cosmic Horror Anthology

Cover art by Mx Morgan G Robles

Edited by Alex Woodroe

Content warnings are available at the end of this book. Please consult this list for any particular subject matter you may be sensitive to.

TENEBROUS

PRESS

Published by Tenebrous Press.
Visit our website at www.tenebrouspress.com.

First Printing, October 2026.

Print ISBN: 978-1-959790-69-3
eBook ISBN: 978-1-959790-70-9

Cover art by Mx. Morgan G Robles.

Edited by Alex Woodroe.

Formatting by Lori Michelle Booth.

All creators in this publication have signed an AI-free agreement. To the best of our knowledge, this publication is free from machine-generated content.

Distributed by Independent Publishers Group.
https://www.ipgbook.com/

Featuring Creators from YOUR BODY IS A FEVER DREAM:

SPLIT SCREAM Vol. Five—novelettes by **Bitter Karella** & Lyndsey Croal

CASUAL by Koji A. Dae, illustrated by **Helen Whistberry**

YOUR BODY IS NOT YOUR BODY—various, a New Weird Horror anthology from trans and gender nonconforming creators

THE SKULL & LAUREL—various, a quarterly magazine of New Weird Fiction

Selected Other Works from Tenebrous Press:

Olyoke by Vincent Endwell

Dear Stupid Penpal by Rascal Hartley

Puppet's Banquet by Valkyrie Loughcrewe

All Your Friends are Here by M.Shaw

From the Belly by Emmett Nahil

Crom Cruach by Valkyrie Loughcrewe

One Hand to Hold, One Hand to Carve by M.Shaw

Table Of Contents

Introduction

Rue Dickey

Becoming yourself is an aching, moulting process. Some parts are bloody; some parts are soft—and some both, like scraping the velvet off antlers. It hurts and it peels and it reshapes until the face in the mirror is yours—really and truly yours. And then all the pain will have been worth it.

The most beautiful part of this process is learning you don't have to do it alone.

My own trans journey was a very personal one that involved multiple breakdowns, every identity under the sun, and a generous helping of self-loathing. I did not always understand I was trans—only that I was different, or wrong. I didn't want to be my father's daughter, I didn't want to be the matriarch, I didn't want to play with dolls. But I also did not find comfort in the pursuits of suburban boys—because I wasn't one of them, either.

It wasn't until I met other queer and trans people—first online, and then in-person—that I started to understand who I really was. It wasn't just about learning the words, it was about learning myself. I learned about myself from friends, mentors, lovers, and abusers; and I learned about myself from the art and words of others, new mirrors in which to see myself.

In every story of this anthology, I learned about myself again.

Body horror and body autonomy are interlocked in a never-ending dance, a sensual and deadly tango. Being trapped in a body that doesn't feel yours is its own horror, and sometimes witnessing the grotesque, bloody peel of skin from bone, you grin and think of how wonderful it would be to shape yourself like that. When the oppression of society has forced you into molds that warped your body and cut into your spirit, losing physical form for the infinite possibility of 1s and 0s feels like flying.

There is nothing I can recommend more to someone looking to explore themself than to read the stories of Black, brown, disabled, queer, and trans people. The way we experience the world gives us new lenses through which we express ourselves. And reading work from a lens that isn't your own gives you perspective you may not know otherwise. I'm not just talking about memoirs and personal essays; I'm talking about the works of fiction and exploration that are flavored by human experience.

Whether a story sticks to the real, wanders into fantasy, or sails through the stars of speculative fiction, there is always an element of truth to be seen. Seeing shades of myself in these stories, I felt a moment of connection with each author and artist. Most of us have never spoken, and likely never will. But a piece of each of them resonates within me now and will color how I move forward through the world.

We are always growing and changing. We are always learning from each other—whether close by or parted by generations. I hope you can see yourself in these pieces as I have and learn new, wonderful truths about yourself. And I hope to learn something new from you someday across the eons.

***

**Each year, myself and my spouse organize a charity bundle that benefits queer and trans organizations doing on-the-ground work in hard-hit states and communities. To join and support these bundles, keep up with us via https://transrightsbundle.space and on Bluesky at transrightsbundle.bsky.social.

Rue Dickey (they/he/xe) is a mixed-race, disabled, nonbinary trans man living on unceded Clatskanie-Kalapuya territory in Oregon. By day, they work in games marketing, and by all other hours, he can be found doing freelance writing, game design, editing, and authenticity reading. Xir crowning achievement is TTRPGs for Trans Rights, a charity fundraising initiative that has raised over $1 million for grassroots organizations serving trans people in highly impacted states.

EAT OR GET EATEN, BABY:
A Two Page (T4T) Fishing (Horrormance) RPG

DAVE V. RISER

Each round begins with a roll of a d8. The number on the die corresponds to a number below. Each number has two or more choices. Choose carefully. You will lose or gain points depending on the choice you make and cannot make choices that take any of your points below zero. After any trades you wish to make, roll the d8 to begin a new round.

You begin the game with: 0 points of BLOOD, 0 points of FRISSON, and 4 points of GUILT.
After your first roll, you may trade 2 points of BLOOD for 1 point of FRISSON at any point. You may also get rid of 1 point of GUILT by discarding 2 points of FRISSON.

If you end a round with 8 points of GUILT, you put the knife down and leave the house. You never return. You can't stop crying. You will never become. The game ends.

If you end a round with 8 points of BLOOD, you will join your dinner. Remove your own gills and sleep a heavy, glorious sleep nestled in the brine of your loved ones. The game ends.

If you end a round with 8 points of FRISSON, you may choose your end: you may shed your heavy human skin and return to the stream you were born into, OR, you may walk to the sea shore and become something brilliant and new. The game ends.

1) You have caught a fish. Its lip swells around the stainless steel hook. Isn't it beautiful?
   No: Throw it back. Ignore the sobbing. +1 GUILT, +1 BLOOD
   Yes: Take it home. Ignore the sobbing. +2 GUILT, +2 BLOOD

2) Scrape the scales off. Hold it down; it's still wriggling. Feel it tremble in your hands.
   Kill it first: +1 BLOOD
   Let it feel: +1 GUILT, +1 FRISSON

3) Cut the gills. It manages to gasp one last thing before you hook your fingers behind the delicate membrane.
   "Please, oh—" +1 GUILT, +1 FRISSON
   "I forgive you—" +1 GUILT, +2 BLOOD

4) Slit the belly open. It's hot and wet inside. What do you find?
   Your missing engagement ring: +1 GUILT, +2 BLOOD
   Another fish: -1 GUILT, +1 BLOOD
   A still-beating heart: +1 GUILT, +2 BLOOD

5) Insert your sharpest fillet knife close to the rib bones. It slides through so easily, coming apart under your blade.
   Do it perfectly: + 1 BLOOD
   Slip. Your blood combines with its: +1 GUILT, +2 BLOOD

6) Cut out the pin bones. You wouldn't want to choke, would you?
   No: -1 GUILT, -1 BLOOD
   There's something sharp in your throat: +1 GUILT, +1 BLOOD

7) Hold the still-warm flesh in your hands. Let the fluid soak your fingers. Your mouth waters. Every part of you is slick. How will you take it?
   Steamed and soft: -1 GUILT
   Raw and dripping: +2 BLOOD
   Pan-fried to perfection: +1 FRISSON

8) How does it taste?
Delicious. It falls apart on your tongue. You've never seen anything so awful or so wonderful. Split open this way, it looks just like—well, you remember, don't you? How it felt when their hands pulled you apart? Their mouth? The hot, wet clutch of throat around you? +2 GUILT, +2 FRISSON
Oversalted. You throw the whole thing away. You don't want to be like them. You don't want to remember. +8 GUILT

The Dark Pouch

Jackie Marley

Editor's note: This account of a notorious early misunderstanding between humanity and the Leute is sure to be an invaluable resource for future diplomatic efforts, given it is one of the few Leute perspectives on the event. Note that though the Leute reproduce asexually, their language distinguishes between those adopting a "hierarchical" and "anarchic" social attitude. This has been translated using male and female pronouns, respectively, throughout.

Greta Kollwitz was the first daughter born to the Kollwitz clan in seven generations. The family's unblemished masculine line had been a great source of pride for her father and grandfather. Though scientific orthodoxy viewed a person's gender-positioning as being determined prior to birth, Greta was, nonetheless, made to feel she had erred somehow. The idea Greta's femininity stemmed from the nutrients she received while gestating in her father's marsupial pouch was a forbidden topic in the Kollwitz household.

The recent arrival of the alien visitors and their disturbing bifurcated sexual act had many people anxiously clenching their cloacas when their thoughts turned to reproduction and the oozing contents of the marsupium. For the Kollwitz's, this discomfort was sublimated into acts of derision toward Greta—mocking everything from the patchiness of the fur on her chest to her inability to digest the tough skin on figs and crabapples. Her three brothers, Leopold, Franz and Ludwig, took their status as preferred children in stride.

The household was geared toward masculine hierarchical pursuits, granting only token concessions to Greta's needs. Once a week, she was deposited in the damp stacks of the local library and told to gather whatever information on "woman stuff" she might need. Meanwhile, her brothers enjoyed a trip to the local climbing gym, followed by their favorite cafe. She spent hours tracing her fingers along the rotten vellum spines, occasionally teasing a book open to breathlessly read an obscure passage.

It was in the library that she first felt the presence behind her forehead. A dense black mass, pressing inside her skull, invisible but heavy, like a hidden planet. From this mass, she felt her emotions and desires drip out, the wellspring feeding her conscious mind; trickles of instinct telling her which books were worth reading, which incomprehensible phrases she should memorize. "The pouch lining is the Leute's only zone of empathy," she had copied down as an epigraph to an early diary.

She had a dim sense of its inner workings, this dark mass behind her psyche, and on summer evenings, when her brothers got bored of forcing her to wrestle with them, she would lie under a mango tree in thick solitude, prodding at it. At times she felt a ripple of insight, provoking an ecstatic rush in her chest, though it was always too delicate to put into words. She sensed that inside this darkness was her essence, a codex to her being that she was unable to decode. Her family, she thought, must have essences at odds with hers, which was why they were compelled to demean her.

In her eleventh year, she was forced to revise her theory. She and her brothers were prowling the housing estates close to their home. As the sun was dipping low, the siblings entered the small patch of woodland that formed a communal play area for the neighborhood children, a clutch of rubber trees with a giant kapok at the center. As they approached, they saw figures on the treehouse platform inside the central tree. Greta was about to veer away to an unoccupied area, but Leopold grabbed her by the arm. She spun into a scrum of her brothers, all bristling with anticipation. They were silently gripped by unanimous agreement. The hair on their foreheads and shoulders bristled out, and they spewed pheromones of violence and excitement.

"Fucking pouch lickers think they can take our tree," Leopold whispered, and the other brothers grunted and smacked their lips.

Greta grinned anxiously and hoped no one was paying attention to her confused scent. Ludwig wrapped his arm around her, whispering some encouragement as he swept her along. The group snuck round the back of the Kapok and climbed up the trunk to a branch overlooking the treehouse.

The siblings looked down on the two boys below. Franz and Ludwig nudged each other, pulling back their lips but unwilling to break the silence. Leopold glared at them both, and they bowed their heads.

"What are you doing in our tree?" He shouted down.

The boys below looked up, smiling at first, then tense when they saw the posture of their antagonists.

"It's a free city," the taller of the boys said eventually.

Franz spat and stared downwards, while Ludwig fidgeted a little. Leopold looked at his brothers, then looked down.

"This is a Kollwitz tree," he said. "So, get the fuck off before I ask a second time." He started slapping his thighs the way heroes did in the movies, though on his pre-pubescent legs, the impact lacked the cinematic resonance. Still, it inspired Franz and Ludwig to launch into a chorus of howling and slapping. The actions of her brothers felt stilted and artificial, but the peaty smell of violent intent was undeniable.

"I said don't make me ask twice," Leopold said.

He grabbed a branch near him and, after a couple of attempts, tore it from the tree, then threw it at the boys below. Greta gasped, though it missed the platform entirely. Franz and Ludwig joined in, tossing handfuls of sticks which pattered down through the branches. The boys below started throwing the debris back up, also missing. Ludwig clambered across to a branch holding a clutch of the Kapok's great nuts and hurled one of these. It landed with a crash on the platform below and everyone fell silent at the violence implied in the sound.

"Psycho," the taller boy said. "We were going home anyway; this park is full of creeps." The pair backed their way to the rope hanging off the platform, puffed out and teeth bared, then slid away.

"You're the creeps," Franz shouted after them. "Your whole family are full-moon perverts."

Greta's brothers started yelling in victory. They clapped each other round the neck and took turns sniffing each other's armpits, inhaling the triumphant pheromones. Greta stayed off to the side, glad they'd forgotten about her. As they hopped down to the platform, the brothers started reliving the confrontation in tiny detail, enlarging the scale of their violence and clarity of action with each retelling. Greta did not share their exhilaration, which was not unusual. What shocked her was the connection the brothers had achieved. They were all of one mind, their innermost desires visible to each other without occlusion. Other people could make themselves understood.

After they had calmed down, Ludwig came over to Greta and squeezed her arm in reassurance. "Don't worry, I know it's a bit silly, but it's just how brothers have to act."

At school, Greta drifted apart from her siblings. Her father had insisted they all attend the family alma mater. The brothers excelled in wrestling, debate, and military history, the school's specialties, while Greta flunked. When puberty hit, she retreated further, shocked at the outbursts of violence and domination that accompanied her classmates' menstrual cycles. Her brothers flourished in this charged atmosphere, all having substantial growth spurts. Leopold established himself as the grade's alpha, Franz and Ludwig his Lieutenants. Greta avoided overt victimization thanks to her brothers. However, though she grew a little, her hips remained narrow and her fur patchy, ensuring she was a nonentity in the school hierarchy.

Art class was the one place she risked extending herself. The school provided such teaching at all as a reluctant concession to the state curriculum and paid little attention to what students produced. Thus, when Greta's class were tasked with painting a portrait of the nation's founder, King Fredrick, she granted herself a freedom of expression she would never have dared in any other context.

While the boys in the class drew a quick stick figure and returned to wrestling, Greta mixed her oils and took the task seriously, attuning herself to fine tendrils of instinct. At first, she went slowly, sketching her plans in charcoal, getting periodically distracted by the violence around her. As she started applying paint, the grunts of the boys jockeying for dominance faded, as did the smell of shredded bark beneath her feet. She depicted

Frederick as one of their prehistoric forebears, naked in a tree nest, a pair of newborns straining their heads out of his pouch, their limpid skin streaked with menstrual yolk. Painting the king's face, she recast that familiar expression of imperial arrogance into a primitive cry for survival.

Greta's oversight was that her art teacher was also an outsider. After years of griping, the economics teacher had finally been released from supervising art class, and the responsibility was outsourced to an adjunct. This woman took the liberty of actively encouraging her students' artistic development. A couple of weeks later, she drew Greta to one side to announce that the painting had been entered into a citywide competition for high school artists and that, having been nominated as a finalist, the work would be featured in a public exhibition later in the month.

Greta felt a rush of shame at the thought of being on show, and bowed her head, her fur flattened against her skin. Over the ensuing days, as she lay ruminating in her sawdust-cloaked attic room, daring ideas crept into her mind. In the painting, she had let her hidden core guide her, its secretions more tangible when released onto the canvas. She'd done so assuming no one else would see it. But someone had seen it and liked it. There were people out there she might connect with.

Despite her best efforts, her father got wind of the show and berated her for associating the Kollwitz name with the world of artists. When he saw the list of dignitaries who were attending the opening, he had a change of heart. He and his three sons entered the oak-beamed ballroom of the modern art museum with chests puffed out. They strode through the gallery in their aristocratic suede gilets, clapping necks with peers and superiors. Greta, in her sagging flannel shirt, shuffled along in their wake.

When her father reached her painting, he flew into a rage. She'd depicted a naked man, with his pouch and joeys exposed to the world, and not just any man, the nation's founder. Dragging Greta into a bathroom, he hissed that she'd humiliated him and jeopardized the prospects of her brothers.

"Since your uncle joined that disgusting full moon cult, we have to be extra careful," he said. "You're basically inviting people to start spreading rumors about us."

Leopold echoed his father's accusations with fraternal

sanctimony, then slapped her in the tender region just above the pouch. The whole family left quietly, calculated enough in their rage to avoid causing a scene. On his way out, Ludwig shot her a sympathetic glance over his shoulder. Greta staggered back into the gallery in a daze. Across the room, she saw a flash of bald flesh. With a shudder, she realized it was an alien. She stood there transfixed but unable to approach it.

The event organizer spotted her and marched over, gushing with superlatives. He introduced her to a couple of art critics, then strode off satisfied. The critics spoke to her in conspiratorial tones about what styles were sure to be the next big thing and offered advice on navigating the art business. After she was back home and the adrenaline had faded, grief sank into her lungs. Those she'd hoped might understand her were concerned not with buried reality but trends, markets and the peccadillos of collectors. Still, the spark of hope she'd felt was addictive. She resolved to keep mining deeper inside herself until she struck a vein of connection.

While the rest of her family shunned her in the aftermath, Ludwig was solicitous. He asked her to design flyers for his upcoming campaign for student president. He had realized that instead of spending all his time trying to win over the alphas, as his rival candidates were planning, he could focus on the school's underclass. Greta's portrayal of him as a man of the people, one arm around a math nerd, the other around a shaggy-coated dropout, sealed his election victory.

Later, when Greta was eking out a living as an artist, Ludwig continued to support her career, introducing her to an agent he'd met at one of his campaign fundraisers. She fast became known as an up-and-comer in the city's countercultural underground. Her exhibitions were held in the old barracks and munitions factories scattered across the city's southern fringes. Troupes of young rebels, with scandalously shaved arms and legs, crowded into her shows, and those with secretly wealthy families bought her paintings.

Ludwig would show up at these events, improbably dressed in his high-society suede, and drink cups of cheap wine with Greta and her artist friends. He enthusiastically joined in with the slurred polemics on the revolutionary potential of his sister's art, making only the most modest and subtle allusions to the reforms he was pursuing in his own career. Greta was mostly silent. Her work was personal; the drippings she'd caught from the darkness in her skull. She had no idea how others connected it to such unequivocal goals.

Around this time, Greta developed a fascination with the alien visitors. She started creating a series of massive collages, combining the limbs of Leute and alien, blended monsters floating free of scale or perspective upon primal landscapes that from one angle looked like the deepest jungle and from another like outer space. These works started to gain wider notoriety, after a reactionary columnist caught wind of them and wrote one of his rote polemics on the moral degradation this exemplified. This led to a couple of art critics venturing from their cocoon in the city center to the sticky warehouse floors of the exurbs to see the works in person.

Greta was featured in a magazine spread, this time for painting portraits of Leute equipped with alien reproductive organs, at times engaging in the multi-person sexual acts that were scandalizing polite society. She even found a stash of books labelled as "smut" within the aliens' library for inter-planetary exchange and reread them compulsively. When she appealed to the alien embassy for more material on this subject matter, her request was denied.

Greta was smarting from the embassy's rejection when Ludwig called. At a gala for his upcoming election campaign, he had introduced one of the aliens to her work. This man, the senior cultural ambassador for the visitors, was enamored, and Ludwig arranged for the three of them to meet. Soon she was having an uncomfortable dinner in an exclusive treetop restaurant with this alien and her brother.

Greta willed herself to engage as if she were talking with any other person, making eye contact and remembering to eat. Up close, the obscenity of the alien's hairless skin and tiny delicate hands that flickered about as he spoke were overwhelming. She felt nauseous and short of breath. She endeavored to describe her work in the terms gallerists used, rather than her usual stuttering thoughts. Ludwig squeezed her thigh under the table in encouragement, but with enough force to convey his resolve.

She left the dinner feeling that she'd failed and was shocked when a letter from the ambassador arrived with a proposal. He wanted her to participate in a joint exhibition with one of the aliens' leading contemporary artists, with the works being displayed alongside each other in galleries on both planets. Ludwig was ecstatic, he was preparing to run for city alderman, and this would draw the media spotlight. Greta was most excited about gaining access to an uncensored archive of the aliens' cultural output across their history. She spent the next month immersing herself in its seedy alcoves.

The exhibition was to be shown in the city's national portrait gallery, the first time Greta's art had been displayed in a central space since the competition of her school years. It was a video work, to be screened for the first time that evening. So, during the initial mingling at the opening, the nature of the show was a mystery. While the aliens were at ease, drinking and over-complimenting the classical art on display in the rest of the gallery, the Leute were on edge, concerned the work would offend or flop or perhaps would not show at all due to technical failure.

Small screens showed the alien artist's work, impossibly crisp images using alien technology which they'd been so far unwilling to share, despite sustained diplomatic efforts. The images meticulously blended iconography from Leute myths and those of the aliens, evoking a shared worldview with just enough subtlety to obscure the underlying sentimentality. All the Leute dignitaries made a point of cooing over them to the aliens. Greta was too tense to have any reaction at all. Propelling her around was Ludwig who quivered with ambition, slapping necks and complimenting guests as he wove through the crowd.

Greta must have had conversations during this period, but she remembered nothing. It seemed an instant after she entered the building that the lights dimmed. She felt a fearful pulse in her cloaca but also relief that things were finally in motion. The audience took their seats in a room now pitch black, facing a blank wall. At first the wall remained dark, then it was struck by a visceral white glare as the projector clicked on.

On the right side of the wall appeared footage of aliens copulating. Though city intellectuals had some familiarity with this act, they understood it in exclusively biological terms: the insertion of one sex organ into the other and the resulting transmission of genetic material. And though they knew there was some associated pleasure for those involved, they demurred from inquiring into the specifics.

Now they were confronted by sex as an ongoing act, the male pounding on top of the female in a protracted manner, with no end in sight. Greta, in her trawling of the alien archives, had uncovered media known as "pornography". The audio was turned up uncomfortably loud, the room vibrating with alien moans and the sounds of belly hitting belly, thigh slapping thigh, the sticky snap as skin peeled apart again, the impact unmuffled by fur, obscene in its clarity.

The camera zoomed in, forcing the audience to stare at images of mouth clamped on mouth, mucous membranes of inner lips, gums and tongues sliding against each other. There was murmuring and fidgeting in the audience as the camera stayed on this unnatural contact for long oily seconds, before the video cut to a montage of new scenes, whirling through displays of the alien sexual organs wielded in ever-changing ways, spinning uncontrollably away from their proper evolutionary targets. Mouths acting upon genitals, then sucking and roaming over the entire body, especially areas of glandular activity; feet, neck, armpits, nipples, and anus. New arrangements of alien, male with male, female with female, huge crowds of aliens smearing together, aliens with anatomies the Leute had not realized were possible. The speed of cuts intensified to a strobing of images, closeups of clitoris and glans penis filling the screen—a kaleidoscope of violent oversaturated colors, pinks, purples, blacks and browns.

The Leute were appalled and started talking over the screening, but as they looked around, they saw that the aliens were smiling and nodding, so they repressed their discomfort in case they revealed themselves unsophisticated. They were so caught up in the shock of what they were seeing that they didn't consider the other side of the wall, still blank.

As the montage of alien fornication continued, images appeared on the left. An aerial shot of a clearing in the woods where a circle of Leute were standing. It was night, and there was a fire at the center; the visibility suggested a fierce moon. The footage was shaky and unfocused, filmed on a handheld camera balanced in one of the overhanging tree branches. The noises of alien sex retreated, and the sounds of indigenous polyrhythmic drumming faded in.

The picture sharpened, showing the Leute rotating around the fire, their hands in their pouches. The audience fell completely silent as they realized what they were seeing: footage of an illegal full moon ritual. The people on the screen pulled their hands from their pouches, slick with fluid. and began rhythmically flicking gobs of viscera into the fire, chanting offerings to gods of the barbaric past. The view switched to a camera amid the crowd, zooming in on animal eyes, bloodied fingers and the black depths of the marsupium. The figures began drawing runes upon their faces and chests with menstrual blood, even tasting it. They sped up their circling until they lost coordination. People collided, rolling around on top of each other. They reached inside the other's pouch, then clasped hands, blending the blood together and smearing it on each other.

On the other screen, bodily fluids erupted; semen, spit and vaginal discharge rubbed on faces, inside mouths, on breasts and hair. The Leute in the woods, meanwhile, had balled into a single knot and now emptied their cloacas, the waste slurry oozing between them. Both aliens and Leute glistened lubricious in their coats of ectoplasm.

Members of the audience started leaving, no longer caring what the aliens thought. Someone had the wherewithal to cut the video feed, and the lights came on. No one spoke and the audience shuffled out. The noises of feet scraping and bags being gathered sounded unnaturally loud. Some of the aliens lingered, seeming interested in discussing the work, and confused at their hosts' reaction. But the hostility in the room soon convinced them to leave.

Before Greta could make her own exit, she felt an arm on her shoulder. Ludwig slammed her into the wall.

"What the fuck are you doing," he hissed, glancing over his shoulder. "You just ruined my career."

Greta froze in confusion. Her brother's fingers were digging into her bicep and felt like they were about to pierce her skin.

"Well say something," Ludwig said. "Was this your plan all along, to sabotage me?"

"I just went where the art took me," she said finally.

Ludwig scrunched his long arm around his face and screamed into the crook of his elbow.

"I thought you knew what you were doing," he said when he lowered his arm again. "You had always pushed right up against the line, titillating the audience, but never going beyond it. This was filth, airing our dirtiest secret in front of the aliens. How could you think it would be a success?"

"But I've never thought about success," Greta said, bowing her head in submission. "My previous work was tentative, because my mind was still tentative. I finally grasped it, though, so I had to show it."

She fell silent and curled down further. Ludwig slammed his palm on the wall above her head and breathed out through his teeth.

He started walking away, then turned back. "Leopold was right. Father should have ripped you from his pouch when he had the chance."

Greta was alone. This hurt, though she'd known all along her brother was using her. Even the underground galleries wouldn't risk working with her now, and in the ensuing years she slid into obscurity.

Her fear and bitterness eventually faded, and what remained was the image of horrified faces when the lights came on. She returned to that memory again and again while lying in lumpy hostel beds, unable to sleep. In that moment, she and her audience understood each other.

It Is No Longer Enough to Die for Love

ELENA SICHROVSKY

[READY FOR TRANSMISSION]
[. . .]
[SIGNAL INCOMING]

Static, sustained. Dial knob turned until click. Squeak of chair wheels, springs creak from seat shifting. Buttons pressed above and below. Volume increasing from the left. A voice, audible despite garbled background noise. Chair wheels roll closer, then stop.

"It just feels like we're being watched . . . no, more like monitored. I'm not being paranoid, trust me, I know paranoid. *[click of a lighter]* This is something else, it's like—don't give me that face. Come 'ere. *[laughing, exhale]* Fine, sit on my lap babe, but look, I'm serious."

***

Your love is going to kill us all.

That's what the Oracles said. You didn't ask. They arrived on the balcony two days after he called you back.

They said, this is how it's going to happen. You love him, of course, but unlike the other ninety-nine-thousand universes, in this one you realize that he loves you back. Has wanted you all along, you lovesick idiot.

Then you lose him. The Oracles don't, or won't, say how. Only that you decimate reality in trying to get him back.

Other people get a wish come true and it's free front-row

concert seats or a surprise snowfall on Christmas Eve. You get an impending extinction event.

***

[T]is sitting on the rooftop of the tower, flipping a lighter back and forth between his palms. It's a mild summer evening, not warm enough to explain the elongated blotches of sweat patterning the side of his t-shirt, or how labored it feels to breathe right now. He hears [S] coming up behind him but he doesn't turn around.

After a moment [S] reaches into his jacket pocket and pulls out a pack of cigarettes. [T] leans over to take one and his knuckles brush against [S]'s fingertips.

S:
So. What happened since the last time I saw you?

T:
What *didn't* happen?

***

They said that the ending could not be forestalled.

You said clearly you haven't met me.

First you tried to remove him from your memory. Immediately after, you tore apart the Appalachian trying to remember him. The second time you altered the recipe to give yourself a seizure every time you thought of him. You foolishly thought pain could deter longing. You ended up crawling into Mt. Vesivus, choking on your own spit before he came and dragged you out.

Why do you get to do all the dramatic gestures, he said. Next time burn me alive too.

You jerry-rigged an atom bomb to blow both of you up on Saturn's furthest ring.

Did you know it's called the Phoebe ring?

That's nice. Very nurse-in-care-home-type name.

Well you are pretty old.

Fuck you too.

***

The corner of the cigarette box folds under the pressure of [S]'s thumb. His throat stings like sandpaper across open sores. The moon is too timid to shine tonight. There's some light from the traffic below, enough to illuminate the crease of [T]'s forehead.

S:
Do you believe—is there any chance that it's actually true?

T:
(passing the cigarette)
I think we, of all people, know that *anything* is possible.

***

[TRANSMISSION INTERRUPTED]
[. . .]
[SIGNAL UNSTABLE]

Steady rhythm of blip noises, then it stops. Chair wheels roll further into the background. Switches flipped, speakers hiss and crackle before emitting a low hum. A dial knob is turned.

"There's nothing to solve here . . . honey, if there was, you'd have figured it out by now. It's not random, either - look, think about it: someone, or something, out there *wants* to do this to us. Because they can. *[sniff, hard breathing]* Maybe they think it's fucking funny."

***

If you both die, the Oracles said, it will still happen.

Not here, not in this time, but somewhere else. The outcome is part of the story now; dust the embers from your palms to scorch a different page.

For the final attempt, you entombed yourselves in separate galaxies. The Milky Way cracked and then bled stars for half a millennium. Turns out that even unconscious, you'd been tunneling towards each other.

There's no uninhabited planet for you to be exiled to. Not when he's looking at you like that. You used to have drunk fantasies about him looking at you like that.

***

Constellations scatter.

[T] dangles a half-smoked cigarette off the crest of his bent knee. [S] watches as the burning end goes out and a thin white trail rises. [T] keeps his eyes trained to the darkness above. The pool of his throat is trembling.

S:
I need to tell you something.[1]

T:
Jeez, that doesn't sound good.

[T] laughs but the noise becomes twisted, ugly. He tries to light the cigarette to mute the sob. [S] gently pushes the lighter down and cups [T]'s face in both hands. The bridges of their noses are almost touching. [S] runs a thumb across his cheek.

***

---

[1] the first weekend we spent together we were in meetings all day and that evening you came over to my place for a movie then we made out for awhile but i was too tired for anything else and i woke up around five to go to the bathroom and noticed the window curtain had slipped open there was a gap and a beam of sunlight speared across the side of the bed you were asleep on remember you were growing your hair out back then and it was splashed halfway across your face and every time you exhaled the strands against your nose fluttered a little i knew then that you would be my only reason for anything i ever did there was nothing i wouldn't do for you *nothing* and i thought it must be terrifying to you to anyone to lie next to a hurricane every night but i don't know how to love quietly and no one prepared me for a world where you love me back

The Oracles are an organism, and as such, they have a threshold of endurance.

He doesn't agree with this. You tell him not to watch. They must know how to end this. There's no knowledge in the world for which there is not a counter.

You do things to them that you wish had never been done to you.

You can be unmade, the Oracles eventually confess. Both of you will cease to exist in nine-hundred-ninety-nine-thousand realities.

What about the one where we do?

They say the thread cannot be entirely unraveled. You'll still be there in the beginning, before any form has ever had meaning. Molecular splinters in a primordial stream that never flows to creation.

Will we—will I know that he's there?

You won't be aware of anything.

But how can I know for sure that he's really there?

What does it matter?

***

[SIGNAL REPAIRING]

[TRANSMISSION TRANSLATED]

Labored breathing, close to the speakers. A voice cuts in and out, unintelligible. Chair wheels warble back and forth. Sirens start to sound. Static burns through, shrill, echoing.

`I need to tell you something.`

`I'm listening.`

Do you know that I've set fire to universes for you? Do you know that I've set fire to universes for you? Do you know that I've set fire to universes for you? Do you know that I've set fire to universes for you? Do you know that I've set fire to universes for you? Do you know that I've set fire to universes for you? Do you know that I've set fire to universes for you? Do you know that I've set fire to universes for you? Do you know that I've set fire to universes for you? Do you know that I've

[end transmission]

set fire to universes for you? Do you know that I've set fire to universes for you? Do you know that I've set fire to universes for you? Did you know that I've set fire to universes for

what spectrum unfurls (beyond)

ACANTHOLICHEN × VARIIFOLIUS

"A source of brilliant light in this deep blackness, [. . .] destined never to witness its own glory."
—William Beebe's *Mid-Ocean,* 1881-1939[i].

1[ii]

The Hadalpelagic zone is the deepest point of the world, named after the god of the Underworld, the origin word Hā́idēs, meaning "unseen".

The spectroscope registers no color, but Dr. Sylmar Methione's orc eyes drink in the darkest blue that goes beyond standardized nomenclature[iii]. The abyss absorbs the memory of the vivid oranges and reds shimmering above his descent through the depths. The sunlight could never again be as wonderful, as yellow faded from green to yield to the overwhelming penetrating blue deepening from ultramarine to azurite, then simply—black. As if it had consumed all the color in the universe.

The two crew members of the *SS Thyone*, a naturalist and an engineer, are the first to sink this far down toward the Earth's center. Until now, the only contact from these unknown depths had been washed up carcasses unrecognizably warped by depressurisation, dissected and diaphonized over the steel tables of their laboratories.

These creatures now dart about, luciferase shimmering beyond *Thyone's* beam, at home between fragments of continents.

So far are they from the light of day and the predictabilities of academic conferences, the hunched ache of examining lab results, squinting at petri dishes.

Now, Sylmar isn't looking through a lens, but the waters encompassing Earth's core. A mere quartz window divides them, fogging with his unsteady breath expelling between slackened tusks. No laboratory could reproduce such conditions.

It was his honor for the dilated void of his eyes to absorb the evanescence of his unseen world.

A thriving galaxy wraps around *Thyone*, with cadmium lights that explode from an ever-moving ghostly membrane.

Stretching the definition of an invertebrate body, ghostly tissue encompasses this siphonophorous constellation, slowly oscillating as it drifts. Network aglow, conserving energy with its gigantism. As the submarine sinks another fifty feet, more layers of lights blink in and out. The liminal ephemerality of a city's twinkling lights under an endless flight into a night that swallows them whole.

The greater the pressure, the softer the tissue.

It reflected in himself the vulnerability of the humanoid body.

The span of this creature across the horizon of the ocean basin cannot be confined to a porthole, imprinted by his bearded cheek. His forehead smears another stamp as he cranes, exclaiming instructions to the pilot for a better vantage in the careening submarine.

What seemed like a flower unfurls luscious feathers comparable to an ostrich's plume, with spines as fluid as eel skeletons, gliding like ribbon. It was hypnotic in the ever curling movement of petals blooming in asynchronous formation, each rippling out to grasp across the water, reaching for the submarine.

Its feathery pinnules ripple as its appendages pull through the water, the motion so unlike the awkward peddling of mammalian limbs.

'Seawater was our original home.'

The effortless grace surrounding a vascular system flowing the water through itself, when his could not.

The seawater their ancestors left is now intolerably saltier with dissolved organisms and minerals, and the pressure here as crushing as an elephant standing on your thumb. Yet this creature glides like silk through water with the grace of a butterfly.

'We are not returning to our ancestral home, but to a place of abyssal unknowns, of creatures arising and passing into extinction without our glimpse.'

Beyond the glass, the creaking submarine is held up to its fascination, yellow spotlights flickering a mere speck of a halo upon the incomprehensible immensity of a god.

The viewports' quartz magnifies the illumination upon the crew—specimens plastered beneath this creature's microscope. If it didn't let go, they would burst through their containment as minuscule particles floating through unsympathetic trenches.

The specimens under the microscope cannot perceive the viewer.

Sylmar only hopes, then, with the barrier of metal removed, in the moments before oxygen would escape his lungs, his last sight could be this creature's sacred grandiosity in whole—unseen by others' eyes.

***

The roar of seawater flooding the narrow confines of the submarine snaps his mind away from reverential death.

Spiny icicles of devouring teeth circle the viewport, and terrible creaking reverberates through the hull.

The engineer scrambles to pilot *Thyone* forward, hollering, "How can we out-swim this eldritch monster?"

Fear bites the base of his skull.

Bells dangling from the creature's translucent mesh trail through view, its flashing illumination silently tolling death through the darkness.

The hull reverberates with exclamations, prayers, barked instructions, and turning gears. But Sylmar stands at that viewport, frozen with the impossibility of looking away, as he takes in its being—and it took in his.

Two creatures from separate worlds, designated by evolution to never cross paths.

'We defied the gods and chose to meet.'

Carmine ribbons drift over delftian blue as they wrap around the submarine. Shaking, squeezing, prodding—like a curious child. Beyond, red streaks like meteorites dance over the twinkling sky of its siphonophorous extensions, and disappear into an infinite blackness, comparable only to naked space between the stars deep beyond the reach of solar rays.

The inarticulable awe of this sight was worth his lifetime

pursuing the mysticism of the unknown, shining brightest in the shadow of death.

Fraught with the inadequacy of words; his heart continues to pump, his lungs inflating and deflating.

But the looming towers of teeth had not crushed them, pulling back from the submarine—a mere morsel to its maw.

Sylmar doesn't doubt it's feathery tendrils could at the very least dent *Thyone* if they squeezed, but they roam and glide along the sphere—

Feeling.

Without sight, it must have electroreceptors in its red tendrils—arms—*feelers*. Sensing the organisms within the odd, unnatural shell of *Thyone* the best way it could.

Thyone creaks, but it has no dents, no fault that signals a damaged exterior.

The creature didn't cause the leak.

Marine life use electric organs and bioluminescence to communicate.

The glow patterns.

"It isn't trying to eat us—it's trying to *communicate* with us."

"Well that's—jolly well"—the elven engineer swears, wrenching a spanner—"but we have greater things to concern ourselves now, if we want to write home."

"It was trying to tell us about the leak we hadn't noticed."

"Don't be daft Methione! These creatures aren't capable of such technical rationale. At the very most it's trying to sense us." He hefted the toolbox into Sylmar's arms. "Now for God's sake, *be useful.*"

2

Back before the Above was even conceived by the Maker Gods, there was only darkness. Time as their tool, they piled layers of silt and salt between the doted creations and the imperfection that came before.

Buried beneath the sea's vastness, the Makers formed the danger of the unknown: Sem'hozisith, 'The Wretched Creature of the Deep'.

The Trench's creatures survive through scarcity.

In the void, there is only isolation, wreck, and snowing decay.

Over years unending as the abyssal murk, occasional joy was found in woodfalls. Unnaturally shaped vessels wrought with planks of hard plants only grown Above, sunk as wreck.

Nourishing the scavengers. Attracting bigger creatures. Feeding Sem'hozisith.

However, the filter feeders cannot consume the metal.

Sem'hozisith would gather the unfamiliar shapes and sharp angles, feelers prodding the compact mechanisms from Above.

These were creations of resourcefulness and innovation. Discards from a society granted millennia to flourish.

As the Gods continued to nurture the paradise Above, Sem'hozisith was forbidden to enter— abandoned and damned by the crushing ascension.

***

Until the little creatures arrive from Above.

The sphere casts electricity in a peculiar focus. Sem'hozisith's electrical senses along their feeding arms tingle at the peculiar sensation of a perfectly straight beam caressing its feelers in a muddied circle. Like an anglerfish's glow, but aimed with the sphere's direction.

Drawn in, the mouths of Sem'hozisith's body-mesh glow in response.

Part of the Trench's environment for so long, creatures that swim around Sem'hozisith's scape behold it as no more than rock spires sustaining algae.

But this sphere *perceives* Sem'hozisith.

Eyes unneeded in a place without light, Sem'hozisith cannot see it. But it imagines that it must be the forbidden holy radiance that the gods created.

Finally, an experience of paradise above.

Its electric senses make out two silhouettes, under the buzzing sphere of rigid lines, electricity steadily swimming back and forth like fish foraging in sand.

***

Now, despite the odd efforts of crafting a shell to keep the unwanted water of the Trench filling the sphere, it shakes like caught prey in death throes.

The creatures inside were shaped like flittering sea angels with their head sending forth electricity atop two busy propelling arms. One broad, one long: firm and tiny like a sunken dolphin carcass. Like baby squid with only four arms which stiffly rotate from torsos.

Flesh angels.

Come from paradise Above.

Eyes and head like telescope fish that stare front, but small jawed and flat toothed. Except the two that jut strongly from the broader one's jaw, like fangtooth fish.

It stands still in Sem'hozisith's direction, yet the other scrambles in their entrapment. It offers a grasping-arm, five points warming the cold obstruction between them, misted by the air brought from another world that escapes its mouth.

Between them, without language, they reckon with the vast unending loneliness between their worlds. Curiosity's thirst for what lay beyond reach, unquenched by the distance between them.

***

The craft tries to ascend.

No.

There was still so much to learn.

Sem'hozisith refuses to be abandoned again.

It tightens its tendrils against the fighting craft's slippery shell. But Sem'hozisith's mind weighs down to thoughts of woodfalls discarded in the silt, the previous life eaten away to leave behind its manmade casings.

Between heartbeats, the currents still; the marine snow freezes.

A creature burrows from the motionless sand, uncurling from its segmented shell.

Electricity buzzes through the water, into Sem'hozisith's mind, voice sliding like laughing eels.

"Halt, Wretched Creature."

"Anak-ta'al." Sem'hozisith's mind-voice echoes along its stem. Drawn out, slow. The drifting mouths along its body-mesh spread the pulses, glowing layer by layer with each echo, down to the sea floor.

Fickle Anak-ta'al is not one of the Makers. But stirs the sand for excrement.

A bottom feeder god.

Smaller than the boulder it scrabbles onto, seeking height.

Fossicking rows of legs scrape at crevices, stuffing into its grasping mouthparts the dust of what died Above.

Sem'hozisith does not have patience for trickery. But Anak-ta'al's magic shifts tides. "Speak."

Time is held leisurely between Anak-ta'al's pincers, "The land-dwellers will die if they don't return Above soon."

"Bring them there. And me."

Anak-ta'al's laughter billows sand. "Your body will be destroyed. Unless . . . "

The silence peels flesh off carcasses.

"I give you a new body."

A pause, but the threads of Sem'hozisith's form remain flowing with the Trench.

"What do you gain?"

"Before mankind was even shaped, before the first fish drew up its fins to walk upon land—the Makers' essence imbued your abyssal vigil." Anak-ta'al's eyestalks devour Sem'hozisith's body. "Give it to me."

But the seabed is never clear. "And what is my cost?"

Anak-ta'al's mind-voice douses a barrier current over Sem'hozisith, uneven cold and salt unsettling its web. Stuttering lights.

"*Desert your making's purpose at adaptation's cost.*
Experience Above, never belonging as one made for it.
Walk on land, yet pain upon each step.
Sight with eyes that burn from forbidden light."

Sem'hozisith wanted to know what flesh could touch, what the Above looked like through eyes, how life flowing through their tube-feet tasted without the salt-thick water.

It grasps for what lies beyond its language.

For if Sem'hozisith didn't, it would drift forever in this silence.

These wretched depths Below can be damned. "Take it. Better than drifting through eternity, abandoned."

Sem'hozisith uncurls tube-feet from its feeding-arms, reaching down.

Anak-ta'al's mouth-legs flex.

A scavenger ready to feast on a whalefall.

***

And then.

Eyes.

Forbidden sight.

Light searing away the deep's oblivion.

Color.

3

Sem'hosizith's name was given by the gods, but it wants a name like one Above. So Sylmar gives it—no, *them*—the name Litian, 'one who finds the light'.

Litian leaves the ocean in their changing sandtracks, dragging roots cut off into two footsteps.

Unsteady against solid ground, there is no current, no flow, only pain. But despite it, elation floats in their chest, breathless in unused lungs even through gasps of foreign air, the salt of home a distant taste on this unfamiliar tongue.

For Litian, who dwelled at the bottom, traversing the layers of pressurized murk to break through the surface—their translucent webbed hands can now reach out to touch the ether without resistance. Mountainous horizons stretch under placid white clouds in an endless expanse of cyan seeping into joyous orange—the *sun.*

Warmth. The holy radiance of life Above blessing their new body.

Beyond is incomprehensible.

Untethered, they feel like they'd fall upwards. What stops their swim bladder from buoying them up?

Sylmar has a kind way of acknowledging their fears: "When you spend your life underneath the sea's layers, all of the limitless surface can feel as terrifyingly, thrillingly, open as the sky."

***

Perfection is a quickly fading varnish upon the Makers' artwork.

The society Above cuts clear borders across land: sectioning fields when squares don't exist in nature, constructing walls around territories not of their own abode.

Binary is peculiar and rigid: either inside or outside, over the fence or within it, male or female. Little room was left for the middle or beyond the narrow scope of its black and white ways.

what spectrum unfurls (beyond)

In the depths, they only had black. But Above, Litian wants to bask in the spectrum of *color*.

> They want the grounding of exposed knees bruised lilac from climbing trees,
>
> jostling shoulders riling their cedar cane to prod crackling sienna embers from bonfires,
>
> rounded cheeks flushing olive as cold ashen lips press to alabaster tusks,
>
> amber-greased fingers tinkering bronze machines to life,
>
> their tired carmine cerata emerging from the pool to tangle through the silver streaking his auburn hairline,
>
> hauling in cerulean tuna between their teeth to deposit writhing at their mate's startled feet,
>
> golden warmth radiating across their torso's empty canvas, stretching over branching veins of violet tendrils,
>
> the gentleness of their scarlet curls spilling beneath an ivory lace veil,
>
> leading *and* being led as they twirl with their husband—vermillion and mauve, pine and champagne—across their wedding floor.

Society confines such experiences to male or female, and administers limits on each gender.

Litian prefers the freedoms afforded to men, but their discrepant appearance provokes discrimination.

Litian is not a woman, but the alternative option prevented marriage to Sylmar.

They make their choice.

***

It is odd how Litian's gender presentation changes the way people talk to them.

With gloves and their face mostly obscured by the welding goggles shielding against streetlights, they manage to hide their most obvious non-humanoid traits.

Acantholichen x variifolius

The alley beside their warehouse was a regular route Litian usually took after closing shop, ambling home with their toolbox clinking against the supportive frame around their grease-smeared trousers. Footfalls less pained with its aid, but would never be as effortless as tendrils through water.

However, tonight, a dress swishes around their clicking bootheels.

A whistle pierces the mouth of the alley, stopping Litian.

A man peels off the brickwork, shrouded in the night, brighter than the dark Litian was used to. "Your boss must be slackin' to make a little lady like you carry his tools."

Litian tilts their head at him, recalling the social script around correcting him.

"Why dontcha smile? Lemme see your pretty face, hun." Alcohol bitters his breath as he staggers closer.

***

An invitation, when most people shied away from the slick gleam of their membrane.

Delighted that someone wanted to see their form, Litian takes off their goggles and smiles—communicating friendliness.

They distend their jaw to let their lips stretch back to their ears, giving a big toothy, spiny smile, with lidless eyes like white headlights in the dim lamplight.

His scream drowns the thud of his shoulder slamming against a hanging bucket of rainwater as he runs.

Pouring it over Litian.

As he scrambles, he trips.

Over the nest of Litian's feet, splayed and elongated into jointed whorls of violet cirri to take root over cobblestone, as their legs seal together to form the stalk of a Sea Lily.

A dozen feathery carmine feeding arms waft down from their crown, a mouth enclosing—to offer him a hand.

"You wanted to see." Without a nose, their voice's confused lilt ruffles from their gills through the translucent webbing along their lengthened neck.

His palms and rear slip on their tube-feet.

"You're not a chick, you're a *monster*!"

Binaries, once again.

***

what spectrum unfurls (beyond)

Gender is to Litian, what the ocean is to one who leaves the shore. Entering the boundless, infinite.

Land dwellers view the land and water with separate borders to traverse. Children are taught to scribble the sea as a solid blue rectangle that stops at the edge of the paper.

Yet water isn't confined to shorelines, crossing beyond the horizon.

The ocean ceaselessly breaks against boulders, spraying seafoam with each wave's attempt to reach the sky.

Dispersed in vapor, consumed and absorbed into clouds, it rains upon the ocean, trees and dirt. Within, the ocean is limitless, unpredictable- containing ridges mountainous and volcanic, while dropping away to the abyssal plains of the world's unknowable hollows.

The ocean is a fluid, changing force that cannot be limited to 'this or that'.

Just like Litian will never be solely of sea or land, bearing features of each. Anak-ta'al was right. They will never be wholly a part of this world.

But Litian will find ways to live around its conditions.

I will find light in myself and through the darkness suffusing the world.

To revere is to love and respect. While the gods eschew it, in this new body I've made my home. I will revere myself and those that love me for all that I am, beyond the bounds of the sea.

[i] Beebe, W. (1881-1939). *Mid-Ocean: Manuscript Material For A Proposed Book.* C0661, Manuscripts Division, Department of Special Collections, Princeton University Library.

[ii] This section takes inspiration from William Beebe's writings, paraphrased in Fox, B. (2023). *The Bathysphere book*: effects of the luminous ocean depths. First edition. Astra House.

[iii] The color standardisation used by William Beebe in the first deepsea expeditions, uses the work of his mentor Ridgway, R. (1912). *Color Standards and Color Nomenclature.*

Feast of Saints

XOSH M. BELANGER

The Monks

They go in, and they come back again, bodies soft beneath coarse-woven robes, their ashen, hairless faces grown strange in the crucible of supplication. With obscenely purpled tongues, they mouth the plainchant doomful syllables of a language fossilized before their grasping forebears could lift themselves from the mud.

Ia! Ia! Ia!

The monks arise from nothing and remember nothing of what came before. What memories they hold are circumscribed entirely by their lives within the temple, from lauds to compline, shuffling through sacramental routine for so many liturgies the ancient stone floors bear soft grooves from the worn habit of their tread.

Twenty-three in all, they each play their roles but are collectively devoted to a singular exalted purpose: nurture the mystery of the Bleeding Saint and, in turn, be nurtured by Her.

The Temple

One hundred and thirty-nine perfect septagons of smoky quartz pave the promenade leading up to the Temple of the Bleeding Saint. The plain beyond is scoured flat by shrieking storms of relentless black sand. Black, too, is the mountain, a brooding plug of dense basalt formed aeons prior at the heart of an extinct volcano. Etched into its sere face is a cyclopean facade of tiered pediments and twined pillars crafted to foretell the inscrutable geometry of constellations long dispersed.

Emptiness reigns from horizon to horizon, and even the endless scream of the sky is beggared of stars. The mountain, and the temple inside it, stand as the final relics of a world whose shape no one living remembers.

No life thrives here, but the monks remain, sustained by the great mystery of the Bleeding Saint: Mother, Savior, Oracle, Provider and prisoner of her own perpetual flesh.

The Saint

"I have a song in me," the Saint declares, then takes the nib of her ink-stained pen and digs, digs, digs until slick globs of orange fat and ribbons of crimsoned flesh pile on the thirsty stones.

Brother Vellum sets aside his writing and scurries to gather her cast-offs. Of the body of the Bleeding Saint, no portion may be wasted. Waste is unforgivable in a barren world.

Cupping the dripping meat in his ink-stained hands, he smells the salty newness of it. His mouth floods as he imagines rolling the feathery scraps upon his tongue.

The temptation is almost too much. To suppress the rising hunger, he sucks his cheeks and sharply bites down. The taste of his own blood gives him focus.

Every morsel must go to the cellarer in preparation for the Saint's Feast Day. Her bounty must always be shared.

Oblivious to the struggles of her humble chronicler, the Blessed Lady continues her self-evisceration. She wears no robe, clothed only in the dark cascade of her ever-growing hair. Blood sheeting across her breasts, she exposes herself to him. Any other monk would be required to look away, but Brother Vellum's role is to bear witness.

"The song," she moans as she drags the pen along her sternum. "You will help me with the song."

He drops his book to the stones. The pages—thick, creamy vellum crafted from the Saint's own skin—fall open to his most recent drawing of her blessed mystery. He is very close to heresy. In all their days together, the Bleeding Saint has never openly addressed *him*.

Her lush thighs churn. First with pen and then with fingers, the Perpetual Lady opens a glistening slit beneath her ribs.

Pushing, prying, gasping as she widens the blood-slick hole, she watches Brother Vellum watching her.

One hand partly inside herself, she extends the other in holy invitation. He cannot refuse. Eager for this communion, Brother Vellum clasps her anointed fingers, and the Bleeding Saint guides him deeper and deeper into her trembling mystery, until her scalding heat surrounds him. She presses his hand to the beating of her heart.

The sacred heart no wound could still.

Her flesh tightens around him, skeins of skin and muscle already reknitting. Such is the nature of the Bleeding Saint. Reluctantly, Brother Vellum withdraws, honoring their moment of shared religious ecstasy by sucking each of his fingers until all her clinging fluids become a part of him. If he commits heresy, it is done in reverence of Her.

As he swallows the last salt-sweet benediction, Brother Vellum startles at the sudden eruption in his loins. Not from shame, but because—for one perfect moment of erotic entanglement—he expects to bear a slit as wet as hers.

The Scribe

Brother Vellum returns to his cell shortly after compline. The tiny room, like every chamber in the vast and sprawling temple, is carved directly from the native basalt of the mountain. There are no tool marks, and the softly rounded edges of the room are mathematically precise.

None of the monks know how this was accomplished.

Cushions and mattress are woven from the hair of the Bleeding Saint, a sacred resource in endless supply. There is no need for crafted furniture. That, too, was already extant, carved from the dense stone of the mountain: narrow bed, low stool in front of a shallow protrusion from the opposite wall, the ledge itself serving as both desk and dressing table.

Brother Vellum reflects, not for the first time, how the monks' cells are each fashioned to match their living proportions — notable because so many other spaces within the temple are dizzyingly huge and unsuited to the shapes of men.

One more mystery in a surfeit of mysteries.

With a heavy thud, he unburdens himself of the massive book he writes in every day— the latest volume of the living hagiography of the Perpetual Lady, their sacred and holy Bleeding Saint. In the days before her feast, it is his duty to shadow her steps, faithfully recording every word and gesture. He is to leave nothing out, for her Scripture is still unfolding.

Brother Vellum has never failed in this duty. Never, in forty cycles.

Never, until today.

Their exchange in her chambers (he can still feel the wet heat of her flesh spasming around his fingers in shared holy rapture)— is not recorded in his book. His ears burn with the omission, but if he chronicles that moment, he will reveal things about himself to the rest of the monastery—things he has striven to hold secret for all time.

I love her. I want to be her.

His rough hands stray to the throbbing under his hairshirt, massaging the stiff urgency of arousal. As he does, he cups his sweating testicles, lifting them away from the blunt stretch of flesh behind. His pen, tip stained rust-red with ink fashioned from the Blessed Lady's blood, beckons him.

The damage she accomplished with a mere pen. The ecstasy.

He longs to plunge the nib into the dense patch of skin and muscle behind his balls and open his own slit. Widen it with his fingers. Fuck it as it slicks with rushing blood.

But he is not their Blessed Lady. He will not miraculously mend. That is her gift, and hers alone.

He holds the sharpness of the pen against himself, daring . . . daring. He's imagined it so many times before. His thoughts retread the fantasy, then his hands perform the act. The taste of her gives him purpose.

With shocking swiftness, he slices the crepey flesh of scrotum. The agony is all-consuming. His legs drop from under him. His fingers continue to work, sawing to free his testes.

Delirious, delivered, possibly dying, he catches the unspooling gonads, pops them in his mouth. Sacrament and sacrifice. Wastefulness is unforgivable in a world so barren. The chamber whirls around him and he chews. They fill his cheeks and crunch and squish, tougher than he'd imagined. The taste of spunk and blood and an underlying bitterness redolent of his strongest sweat almost overpowers the white-hot shrieking pain.

He swallows as his mind sinks away. He does not expect to wake.

***

As the iron bell sounds for matins, Brother Vellum rouses, pasted to the floor in a rank pool of dried blood.

He whispers a prayer at the miracle of his survival, then quickly seeks between his legs. A miracle there, too. One that disappoints him.

His testicles have returned.

The Sign

It is the Feast Day of the Bleeding Saint. The one day no one would bother themselves over Brother Vellum's absence, for he is not required to attend her as she is prepared.

Brother Vellum misses lauds and matins. He skips their meager breakfast. Brother Wish or Brother Branch will notice soon enough, but he needs some space to think and wash away all the crusted blood. The cyclopean stone halls of the temple are winding and vast, but every step is a memory, and he knows exactly where to go.

Down, down, deep into the hushed heart of the temple, past the mushroom gardens, the processing rooms, cistern, and crypts. Down to a massive chamber touched only lightly by whatever inscrutable artifice shaped the towering pillars of their home.

Here, in a space so large the mind can barely hold it, is a miracle as improbable and enduring as their Blessed Lady herself. For here sprouts the eternal rose.

In the center of the chamber—a vast obloid cavern in the basalt—a massive, tangled rose bush rises from a milky crystal round and smooth as river rock. The white stone, stark against all the black basalt, is as big as a table and split neatly down the center. The rose bush rises from this crack, and a gentle stream of water issues just below. Clear, cool, mineral-rich, this deep source of water feeds into the temple, sustaining all the monks.

A single shaft of light—soft white and utterly impossible in a world devoid of sun, moon, and stars—pierces the vaulted ceiling of the chamber, issuing from a source none of the monks have ever divined. But the ageless residents of the basalt temple have learned not to question its miracles, because without this constant light, angled perfectly to fall upon the blessed bramble, the rose bush would not bloom.

They eat the crimson fruits and flowers, use the thick, woody canes to fuel their hearths, they even find uses for the leaves. In the Temple of the Bleeding Saint, nothing is wasted.

And, like the Bleeding Saint herself, the rose bush endlessly renews.

Once inside the chamber, head up-tilted to the glimmering spear of light, Brother Vellum recites a whispered prayer. But the prayer holds for him no answers, and the light only stings his eyes.

Whatever hands shaped this place before left most of the cavern untouched, but their craft is seen in a subtle splash pool arced around the white stone. This guides the water away from the rose bush so it will not drown its roots. A rounded trough—gradually deepened over countless cycles by the water's passing—leads out of the cavern, following a slight incline to chambers deeper still.

Before stepping into the shallow water to wash the blood from his hairshirt and thighs, Brother Vellum kneels on the edge of the splash pool. He meditates on the miracle of the rose and the water, the light and the Perpetual Lady Herself.

And he is overcome—but not with religious fervor.

Before he fully processes his actions, Brother Vellum throws himself upon the boulder and licks the moist crack in the milky white stone. He shoves his face into the crevice, can barely think of anything else. The water is cold, sharply mineral, and kissed ever so lightly by the sweetness of rose.

Panting, he reaches between his legs, imagining the split is there, too, licking harder and more urgently as he massages himself until the water carries both the blood from his unmade mutilation and a fresh spill of seed down to whatever secrets coil in the mountain's hidden depths.

Lips bruised, tongue rasped raw, he rises drunkenly, mouth tasting of blood and stone. To steady himself, he grabs one of the thick, clinging roots.

As he does, a spasm passes through the miraculous rose. The

crimson of the flowers flows backwards into their stems. Blood weeps from the scythed tips of a thousand thorns, and all the roses turn white.

Brilliant petals drift around him, perfuming his skin.

He has chronicled the oracular outbursts of the Perpetual Lady long enough. He recognizes the sign and welcomes it.

The Feast

This is how to prepare the Saint for her feast:

For five days leading up to her feast day, the Saint shall have free access to all chambers. She is attended by her chronicler and encouraged to do as she pleases. She is fed water of rose petals and washed nightly in the same. Any offerings she makes of herself must be dutifully gathered and processed for the feast.

The night before the feast, the Saint must sleep. She is fed a mash of black-gilled mushrooms, the ones called Dreaming-Awake. When the bell sounds for lauds, the Saint is washed with rosewater again. Her hair is shorn down to the scalp and all its bounty collected.

After the bath, the Saint must drink a tea of Dreaming-Awake mixed with the orange-frilled mushrooms called Pain-Calls-Me-Hence. Throughout her final preparations, the Saint may drink of this tea for as long as she is able. It will not spoil the meat.

[[there is a chart with detailed butchering instructions, names for each part and page number references for suggested recipes]]

Flay the Saint in large, intact pieces, leaving her face untouched until the last. The flayed skin should be delivered immediately to the brothers of the tannery, all except the face which will be preserved for the Hall of Seemings. When carving the Saint for the feast, place each portion in its appropriate vessel: fat with fat, meat with meat, tendons with tendons, and each organ dressed separately.

Do not crack her bones for marrow and do not sever her vocal cords. The Saint must be allowed to scream.

Sometimes, she will sing.

At the feast, place the bones of the Saint in all their naked glory at the center of the table. Before and after every course, you will address her and give thanks for it is through her miracle that we have bounty.

When the feast is concluded, gather all the leavings, down to the last dripping. Nothing must be wasted.

With solemn procession, lift the skeleton of the Saint and carry her to the Hall of Seemings. Place the Saint in her sepulcher, the pediment above adorned with her most recent face. She will lie in state for seven days, after which time she will emerge whole again, for this is the nature of her mystery.

Rose

Beside the Saint's sepulcher, Sister Rose waits, keeping vigil with a patience honed through forty cycles of attending the Perpetual Lady's every waking word. In her lap is a book of bound vellum, slimmer than the last, for this is a new hagiography.

As new as Sister Rose.

Before her eyes, the Bleeding Saint reconstitutes. Much of her muscle has reformed and blood runs sluggish in her veins. It's still possible to see the mystery of her heart fluttering behind imperfectly sealed ribs, its furtive beats slowly recalling a steadier rhythm.

From a long slash in her arm, Sister Rose draws more blood for her pen. Like the flesh of the Saint, her wound knits even as she watches, so she works swiftly.

She begins with the traditional phrasing.

Meat we are and meat we shall become.

Her pulse quickens as she shares what yesterday she thought as heresy and today knows is holy revelation.

All hail the Blessed Lady, endless provider, living relic, and mystery of perpetual flesh. She changes everything, and everything is changed through her. We eat her flesh so we may become her. Her body, through our bodies, embodied again.

Sister Rose does not yet understand everything, but the same holy fire gripping her loins kindles in her heart and in her mind. The miracle lies before her and in her. She grips the curling bounty of her hair as proof. It smells like flowers.

All the monks of the temple are bald, and have been since time immemorial, pates barren as the outside world.

Sister Rose is no longer barren. Her body is lush and fruitful. Her flesh, like her hair, continues to grow.

But she is not yet perfect. She must beg for one more benediction, the ultimate gift from the Bleeding Saint. Every time she cuts away, her old self stubbornly grows back. And in a dream before morning prayers, the answer came to her, so right and true, she woke to the hot spilling of seed.

Sister Rose knows what she must do, even if she doesn't fully understand it.

From the depths of the sarcophagus, eyes reform, still lidless, but the muscles anchoring them to her sockets twitch toward Sister Rose. The former chronicler leans eagerly closer, pressing naked flesh against the cold lip of polished stone.

"You wanted to share your song with me," she whispers, wondering whether the miracle of their Saint requires ears to hear. "I understand you now."

Eyes that cannot blink lock onto hers. Sister Rose is filled with holy gnosis.

She holds the bloody pen aloft. Across the knitting musculature of the Saint's chest, nubs of breasts form, knots of veins and glands gathering orange globules of fat around them, layer by layer.

"Do you bless me with this sacrament?" Sister Rose begs.

Unfinished lips twist above exposed white teeth. The Bleeding Saint fails to speak. But she nods. Sister Rose waits, just to be sure.

The nod comes again.

The half-formed eyes of the Perpetual Lady never leave Sister Rose as she slices. Reverently, the former monk lifts the bloody benediction and opens her body like a reliquary. With screams of holy ecstasy, Sister Rose roots the breast-buds against her own wet, exposed ribs.

This is my body.

Sister Rose exults as she experiences the mystery. It knits and swells and grows inside her. Orgasms come in wave after wave, driving her to her knees.

As the preserved face of the Perpetual Lady watches over her, Sister Rose makes her final sacrifice, driving her fingers deep and riding her own rapture until this new shape is all she ever was.

TRANS-ASCENDANT

EMILIJA VAVIC

It began as a lump in my left breast.
The pressure of the machine still a phantom
shroud on my body when the doctor
quietly gave me the results.
"It's nothing to worry about yet,"
 she said,
"we just want to be thorough."
I was already worried, of course,
but not as worried as I should have been.

The dreams began a week later.
Floating in a haze of sensation, like
drowning in the watery realization of life.
Kaleidoscopic darkness made of more than black—purple, violet,
    indigo, orange-blue.
I moved in every direction at once—
there was no true direction here—
through this sea of nonsense sights and smells.
Wings grew from my back
in ripping, tearing jolts out of
my skin like a tree sprouting
from dirt in a time-lapse.
"SOON," a voice called out from
every direction and no direction
at the same time.

Emilija Vavic

"PREPARE THYSELF," it said, a reverberating,
rasping, inhuman thing.
I flapped my new wings—feathered
and scaly, flinging fresh viscera around me—
I asked,
"Can I wake up now?"

The follow-up appointment—
Lab results reflected in the doctor's
glasses as she read
from the screen in her hands—
I couldn't comprehend her resolute,
soothing voice.
There were words like "metastasized," and "double-check," and
"family history," and "hospital,"
and
and
and
"SOON," and "PREPARE THYSELF,"
and I said
"Can I wake up now?"
And the doctor sighed and said
"Counseling will be important."
How long until the hospital?

I awoke in a bed. My own.
No hospital stay. Yet.
My phone shows 2:24 AM.
Nausea keeps me company.
Sick and alone and awake.

I dream of the infinite world of purple, violet, indigo, orange-blue.
A table and two chairs and tea-set
on a placemat before me.
I take a seat, my wings scraping
on the wood of the chair.
I pour the tea for myself.
Hot. Steam. Cinnamon.
"Alice in Wonderland," I say.

TRANS-ASCENDANT

"Why is a raven like a writing desk?"
I giggle at the nonsense of it all.

Fluorescents and antiseptic,
Latex and nitrile and paper sheets.
I miss the dream. There is no
color here. No wonderland.
There were other appointments—
other tests and treatments—but
my weakened flesh caught more than
cancer, like a pool net scooping
up the diseased debris
others leave behind.
The lump had grown exponentially
like one of those algebraic charts
from school. Rise and run. What is the slope?
Bad, I guess.

I hide the worst from
the nurses. When I scratch my side
scales come off. The world
is shifting its color palette, gradient of purple, violet, indigo—
I'm awake. I'm awake.

The nurse reads my chart. He smells
like cigarettes and spiced cologne.
A welcome change to my sterile
surroundings. His hazel eyes glance at me
and he gently says,
"Prepare thyself."
I can't breathe. "What? What
did you say?"
"We're starting you on fluids."
He smiles up at me.
I'm awake. I'm awake.

2:24 am. Quiet hum of machines.
I'm scrolling on my phone. Ads
for health insurance companies flash

by my eyes. The television plays Gordon
Ramsay repeats. Fighting for my life
has never been so boring.

Silence. The machines stop, screens
gone dark. My phone has no signal.
The TV is frozen, a British chef stuck mid-shout.
I press the nurse call button—
The lights go out. I wait.
No nurse. No one comes.
My side hurts. I press my hand
to my side under the gown and feel
rough scales along my breast and ribcage.
It spreads like an oil spill
creeping along the surface of an ocean.
I stand next to the bed
and use my phone to light my side.
The scales are small and rounded,
iridescent and shimmering with an indigo undertone.
I'm awake. Pain radiates from two points
on my back, a sensation
of growth and blistering skin.
I'm awake. The light outside my unit flicks
on, the blank grey desk uninhabited.
I tear at the cords and needles of IVs, free myself
from them in bloody convulsions.
I run to the desk and lean on it for support—
There is no one on the floor.
There are no patients in the units.
I am on an island of fluorescent
solitude.

Far down the hallway, another
light turns on. Purple glow
bathing the stark, clinical hall.
Further down, another light—
violet.
The fluorescent above me
shatters in its casing

with a pop. My breath is
sharp and shallow. The scales have
spread down my arms and cover my hands.
I run to the beckoning light. I can
wake up if I can escape
this dream. Purple—
I trip over a wheelchair—
violet—I don't stop as the lights lead me left down another hall—
indigo—the splitting sensation on my
back has ceased—the double-doors
to the oncology ward swing open—
behind them—
orange-blue.
I limp inside.
The buttons are gone save one:
ASCEND
I stare at it.
The speakers crackle and cough
and play the voice from my dreams—
"PREPARE THYSELF."
I press the button.
It glows orange-blue.
The elevator lurches upward and—
"THOU ART BECOMING,"
"THOU ART BECOMING,"
"THOU ART BECOMING."

My feathered wings surround me and I realize
that I'm awake.
I am awake.
The elevator stops and sends me
sliding to the ground. The floor counter reads
ASCEND.
The doors open with a
ding.
The kaleidoscope of
purple—violet—indigo—orange-blue
swirls before me.
I flap my wings as I rise.

Emilija Vavic

The pain is gone.
My body is strong.
At last I am prepared.
I step into the world without
direction and I run.

All Her Rows of Teeth

JORDAN KURELLA

The dive goes poorly from the start. Within an hour of cutting the engine, the radar can't pick up either the Vice Shark's signal, or Allysandra's. And I need both, if any of us are gonna see land again. So, because Allysandra was wild enough to go searching after the Vice Shark, I gotta go searching after Allysandra. Not because I still love her, but because she's worth millions—millions of millions—and I can't lose that kind of paycheck.

The blip of the radar hits at the tip of my frustration.

"There, Caleb, there."

The captain doesn't have to tell me twice. Already in my overwrought gear for an overwrought dive, the riggers double-check it quickly before I figure out my mask and fall backward into the ocean after a woman worth thousands of memories, and a shark whose legend spans deeper than all its rows of teeth.

***

Not long ago, Allysandra re-found me in my favorite bar on the outskirts of Nowhere, Georgia looking like she belonged there. She always had the talent of looking like she belonged. Wearing an old Rolling Stones t-shirt soaked from humidity and hair just as outdated. Her walk said every bit that she was careful though: about who she talked to, where she sat in a room, and what she drank. And what she drank was soda direct from a bottle.

"Caleb, you look like shit."

She swigged her 7-Up like it was beer. I admit, when I was younger, I'd been attracted to that kind of confidence, but I didn't know Allysandra then.

"What else did you expect?"

Allysandra leaned back in her chair like she owned every inch of the place. She probably did. I smiled, my grin full of porcelain teeth—teeth she paid to put there. Her own grin was full of stains from a life living on the edge. We had matching smiles a while back, there had once been photos of us smiling together. But those probably got destroyed, along with me: Versions One and Two.

"So, anyway, Caleb. Remember all that talk about the Vice Shark?"

"Oh yeah," I said, sipping my own RC Cola, also direct from the bottle.

Now Allysandra leaned in. "What if I told you that I know where it is, and I can lead you right to it."

"Bullshit."

But I'd said it too loud, and too many people were interested. Eager to be a part of this long-lost legend. So long-lost that the Vice Shark's story had been buried in *Weekly World News* microfiche and the Internet Archive. Both told a story of a shark that fed off the most debaucherous hedonism, the dregs of humanity: people like me and Allysandra; people like all of us stuck in Nowhere. And the story goes, if you were lucky (or unlucky) enough to find the Vice Shark, you got one wish.

The trick was finding it: the wish or the shark.

So, like everyone else trying to listen in, I kept my voice low when I said, "Also, why tell me? You contacted me like what—a month ago—after six years of silence? Not since the last surgery. Not since that *One More Party, Please, Caleb* party to see me off. Why the fuck do you want me on this job?"

Allysandra leaned over and put her hand on mine. Her perfect smooth calm fingers covering up my twitching ones. Twitching from nerves and annoyance. I didn't like this, and I didn't want Allysandra here.

"Caleb, you know why. You know why."

"You don't owe me anything, Allysandra. I'm the one who owes you."

She smiled then and stood to leave. But she didn't go; she was waiting for me. I hesitated a minute, then a minute longer. Allysandra knew me too well, but I knew her just as well: the Vice Shark was bait.

Allysandra was leading me to something else.

All Her Rows of Teeth

***

Diving into the murk this far out where the water is mean? That's my favorite. This far above the Mariana Trench, is enough danger to get lost in, enough worry not to get anxious over. This is the Death Valley of the ocean: I am stupid enough to come all the way out here, brave enough to dive here, and desperate enough to go after something like the Vice Shark. Or at least I was, but I'm not that guy anymore.

Allysandra used to *understand* me like I understood her. Because she was me at one point: because I was the girl who studied marine biology at undergrad with her, partied with her, and followed the smell of her $30 hairspray around like it was better than cocaine. Which we both knew wasn't true.

Then, I transitioned. And I kept on with the drugs, I got a boat, and started taking people out on dives. Because international waters were a thing, and drugs didn't matter out here where the water was lawless. On the waves that I could navigate while half-sober while everyone else partied, puked, and nobody died.

Until they did.

Allysandra Fayden and I had grown apart after graduation, because she had a penchant for being bad on a big dime with women who did the same. And I was a guy who played risk with fewer zeroes. But Allysandra had always had a death wish, and one day she came around, and that's how me, Version Two disappeared.

She whispered to me that night, out on the water, under the stars. Everyone was asleep, the party left to damp confetti on the deck and bass thumping in the background. Allysandra and I were still awake and sobering up, finally. I'd only agreed to take her out here after a long reconnoiter. After three of months of fucking in her apartment, and promising that everything was like it used to be. After four months before that of me being a tourist in her life while she showed me how she lived.

That night, though, on the water, when the moon was setting and dawn was threatening, after promising me everything between us was all alright and would always be, she whispered, "How would you like to kill a billionaire?"

I didn't answer. Just fucked her on the prow till the sun came up. Best sex of my life.

Unfortunately, she didn't die. Other people did. It was Allysandra's fault, and she spent a shit-ton of money hiding the evidence: boat sunk, bodies gone. And me? I'm not who I was. Name? Changed. Dental records? Gone. Nose? New. Cheekbones? Smashed and reworked. I got transplants, plastic surgery, and lost my captain's license. My lifeline to being Caleb Gall is dedicated to Allysandra Fayden, delivered to a P.O. Box in Nowhere, Georgia in unmarked bills. I became me, Version Three.

Used to think Allysandra only pretended to be in crime. Truth was, she was. Deeply.

Now, I'm chasing her like I always did, churning in the wake of her destruction because I have no other choice. If she dies, I die. If she goes, I go. Whatever she says, I gotta do. That's how it worked when we were eighteen and that's how it works now. I'm too old for this, and if she's chasing her death wish down here with the Vice Shark, so am I.

***

In college, Allysandra was intoxicating, the drugs she got her hands on were intoxicating. Everything about her: the way she talked, the way she drove, the stories she told, all intoxicating. Just breathing in her secondhand life made me high. The way she walked was a sway, like the wind didn't blow unless she told it to. The way she turned was *en pointe*. I didn't want to be Allysandra, I wanted to be with Allysandra, for the rest of my life. And fuck, did I try. Did I try so hard.

But Allysandra couldn't be tied down to anything for more than ten minutes without wresting control back. Even when she hired me to get the shit to sail all the way out to the Mariana Trench, to find the Vice Shark, she had to oversee every detail. I didn't sign off on anything, I just pointed at what I needed on the computer screen, and she took it from there, her face as unreadable as a seagull's. Her eyes as mean, and as hungry.

This is what I am thinking about as the crew lowers me down farther and farther into the dark water. The suit I'm wearing is rated for impossible dives like these. The deep deep fucking dives when people are going where they really shouldn't. And I've got the captain in my ear feeding coordinates into my HUD of Allysandra's last location. I have about fifty meters before the water gets too cold for the suit to function.

All Her Rows of Teeth

The blip on my radar says Allysandra is twenty meters below me. Her vital signs are low, going lower. She's also not moving. My own vitals spike and the access line to the boat tugs, I tug on it twice. Letting them all know I'm fine. But they're right to be concerned. Those guys have my best interests in this. They hate Allysandra as much as my life with her is complicated. I should leave her behind, leave her down here to die. Boo hoo, big accident, big whoop.

But I never was that smart.

***

I was once obsessed with the Vice Shark. Back when I was getting clean and looking for a new fix to supplement my old ones, I got really into conspiracy theories. Things like birds are government drones and stuff like that. The Vice Shark, though, had always been a fascination. It was unprovable, irrefutable. No one had found it and lived to tell the tale, except for an old forum mention from the late 1990s that ended with: *There Always Has To Be A Vice Shark. Always.*

The legend was basically dead. No news online or anywhere for over a decade. I never said a damn thing; was always good at keeping secrets. But surgery is one helluva deal breaker. Because coming out of anesthesia after my last facial reconstruction surgery—the one Allysandra paid for because of her massive murder fuckup—I blabbed everything.

When I woke up, she was shaking me: "What do you mean, there's a hedonistic shark in the ocean that grants wishes?"

"What?"

"Caleb, this shark that grants wishes: I need it."

"Allysandra, that's my one thing. You have everything, you owe me."

She locked the door of my hospital room and switched off our phones. In my weird post anesthetic clarity, I noticed that her nail polish was chipped; it was never chipped. Her eyeliner was smudged; it was never smudged. Her tone was furious and strained and tired, and she looked basic. Like only a couple thousand bucks.

"I owe you? I owe *you*? I just saved your entire fucking life, Caleb Gall."

"You owe me at this point. Like a lot. Like *a lot* a lot. And this hedo shark or whatever is the payment. Give it to me."

I tried to rub my eyes and she grabbed my wrists. "Don't, the skin graft is still fresh. Anyway, what's it called?"

"Vice Shark, and you're not going without me. Deal?"

"Deal."

***

I reach Allysandra quickly. The HUD hasn't had time to fully set up, but it's fine; it'll be fine. She still has vital signs, but barely. Her O_2 cord is wrapped tight around her arm, and something's shredded her access cord to the boat. Guess that's why the weird signal. Gently, I unravel her O_2 cord, watching her eyelids flutter behind her HUD, which is flashing red and is way unhappy.

So, I do what any contentious friend with benefits would do, I shake her.

Allysandra wakes up and looks at me with wide eyes that are dark and wrong. Her HUD blinks all the warnings, reading all sorts of wrong things; while mine is calm, like everything is fine. But I'm not. I'm panicking, and she's gripping my arm tight.

She grins with too many teeth, and brings up a gloveless hand that I recognize too late is not a hand. It severs my access cord with a single swipe. So much of Allysandra is inhuman now. Her hand, all her rows of teeth, her eyes. And Not-Allysandra grabs me and pulls me to her.

We plunge down, together. Down and down, sending bubbles from my rebreather up way too fast. My unsynched-HUD continues to read everything as just peachy, thanks. Not-Allysandra's display is red and angry. Total red alert, which at least thankfully conceals all her teeth as she smiles at me.

***

When I was me, Version Two, I thought I had a good life. Could do whatever I wanted. Live lawless, which is what my clients wanted. Anything goes. That was the name of my ship: *Anniething Goes*. I was not exactly an attractive man. Too tall, too skinny, too wiry to be truly handsome. The last guy anyone wanted to do anything sketchy with, especially hiring me to captain a boat for their fuckups in the deep water.

But then I found the right clients, and the reviews were five stars all the way down.

When I was me, Version One, I didn't have a good life. Everything was an adjustment. My clothes, my hair, my eyeliner.

Everything I said was too much, too loud, too brash. Too everything. I didn't like a damn thing about me, so when I learned about what transgender was, and applied it to me, it was such a relief, allowing all that too muchness to occupy the right face, the right body, the right hands, the right smile.

Even though that version was Allysandra's favorite, I couldn't ever live up to her expectations of who she wanted me to be. I couldn't ever measure up to what she wanted, her ideal of the woman she wanted me to be. I didn't have the income, the pedigree, the gravitas. Or the tolerance. Either for her lifestyle, or for her.

Me, Version Three, suits me. I'm more attractive, though still kind of weird looking. Being in Nowhere, Georgia suits me. Hanging out in the bar I like suits me. Drinking RC Cola from a bottle suits me. Being sober suits me. Playing the same song on the jukebox suits me. Occasionally playing pool badly suits me. I like being single and I like being alone.

And now this me—Version Three, the one I like best—is being dragged down too fast, too hard, to the coldest darkest meanest part of the ocean, by Allysandra. The woman made this version. The woman I owe my life to, and the woman I chased around my entire life, never measuring up to. Also, the woman who spent her entire life—at least the life that I've known her—trying to die.

In my head, Not-Allysandra's voice comes in with too many s'es, "Caleb, you look like shit."

My teeth chatter as she holds my arm, my heart beats too fast and too cold. My vision starts blurring as her face warps beyond her flashing red display. Her grip tightens, her descent quickens. The water is so dark it's like bathing in fear. Blips of light come from here and there as the water lights up with angler fish and other things with too many teeth and similar vendettas. I want to answer her with something clever, something fun. But all I can say is.

"Well, what did you expect?"

And then the water gets too dark to see her face.

***

In my wildest drug-fueled dreams, I had Allysandra's life. Her closet, her cars, her stock portfolio. But she always told me, "You don't want that. You definitely don't want that. They'd hate you.

They'd hate every word that came out of your mouth." So I learned quickly to stop wishing for that sort of thing. Spending time with Allysandra in New York was a lesson in how bizarre her life was, and how weird she was to hate it. She'd spent every gasping breath trying to be something, someone, *anything* else.

And here she is: that something else. Looming over me, helmet off, face changing. So many teeth and blackening eyes. Skin going grey and losing its pores. I am still in my helmet. The HUD lamp lights up, but the readout lies to me, saying everything is going to be fine, Caleb. Just lie still. Just breathe. Just breathe. You are going to die here, it's fine. It is fine.

"We can be here together, Caleb. You and me, finally. Just wish to be me."

This weird Not-Allysandra is not the friend who'd spoken in a half-smirk her entire life. Her mean-girl special. Now her mouth is too wide, taking up too much of her face as her not-hand strokes the side of my helmet. I'm officially freaking out. My heart beating in my throat, I am going to die here. Die while Not-Allysandra holds me down to the ocean floor with my head dangling over the edge of an undersea trench.

"Just wish to be with me."

This is what I wanted for so long, right? This is what I wanted since I was eighteen and followed her around campus. Jumped into the passenger seat of her car. This is what I had wanted since she asked me to kill her. This is what I've wanted since accepting her paychecks. But now? None of it, none of any of it, is appealing.

So, I ask, "What happened to your face?"

"I made my wish," she says in my head again. "I *became* the Vice Shark."

She pushes me closer to the edge, where the hot air filters up like a whisper of malice. Her grin widens with too many teeth. Worse than the smirk. This is not how I wanted to die—and I will, unless I do what she wants. I hate her even more.

"I want you to be the Vice Shark, too. Caleb, we've always been together, you and me. Don't kill that now."

Not-Allysandra isn't lying to me, my surroundings aren't lying to me. My body feels numb, drugged. Like I'm coming down from MDMA and now all I want is to be one with the concrete. Except it's not concrete, it's the ocean floor. And I'm not partying with my friends. All I have is Allysandra-the-Vice-Shark. She's brought me down here so she could do what she wanted.

The thought hits me like shock.

It's been decades of doing Allysandra's thing. In college, I did what Allysandra wanted. All the time, every time. We went where she was going, I took the classes she chose. Dated the boys she thought were cute. The only part of my life that was truly mine was transitioning, which she was wholly against, until she heard about my business.

Then she found me useful again, I guess. For this.

The shock sends my HUD into full compliance, my eyes wide and me hyperventilating. Allysandra-the-Vice-Shark pushes my torso so volcanic heat hits my back. It feels like her breath steaming up my mask.

"Say you want it." Full of spit and fury, through all her rows of teeth. "Say you want it, Caleb. Say it and I'll let you live."

"I want it." It's a lie. I have to lie to live. "I want it, I want to be with you, Allysandra. It's all I ever wanted."

Part of it is true. Had been true so many times. For so many years I wanted to be with her. To be around her, experience her life, be seen with her. The mention of her name got me clout and clients; talking about my life with her got even more clout and more clients. But that life is over now, and I like being a nobody in Nowhere, Georgia. I just like getting her paychecks. I like not being around Allysandra Fayden. I like being me.

"Wish it," she says. "Wish it, Caleb Gall. Say it."

But I'm panicking. "Say what?"

"Say, you know, 'I wish,' and then the rest."

I'm busy trying to pull myself off the edge, but Allysandra-the-Vice-Shark is very strong. She could easily toss me over this sea cliff, and I'm pretty sure my ability to swim is nil. With a flick of her arm, I can go sinking into that hellmouth of bleak water.

"I wish . . . " I pause.

I don't want to do this. I don't want to play her games anymore.

Allysandra-the-Vice-Shark shakes me. "Come on, say *I wish I could be you.*"

"What if instead I say, 'I wish you could have my wish so you could say it.'"

Allysandra-the-Vice-Shark is furious, and in her fury pulls me to all her rows of teeth. We're face to face, her black eyes search me for trickery. My HUD screams in my ears. I'm both low on oxygen to breathe and fucks to give.

"Caleb, just say, *I wish I could be you.*"

And Caleb Gall dies right then and there.

***

Or at least Version Three dies. The boat pulls him up. His face matches the ID and all the documents I left behind in case something like this happened. Allysandra paid for these fake documents and now she gets to use them to prove Caleb's death. Drowning, terrible way to go. His helmet was gone, gloves ripped to shreds. Allysandra was missing, presumed attacked by whatever got to Caleb Gall's suit, which was likewise ripped and mangled.

I survive, though.

When Allysandra-the-Vice-Shark became me, the transformation was instantaneous. In the mask's reflection, I watched her face become mine, the rows of teeth become those perfect porcelain teeth. I watched the face become mine as it choked and drowned. I watched her swim upward in panic.

The freakiest thing, though, was watching that face in the mirror die. I helped her almost to the surface, until she stopped moving. Then let her—him—her float the rest of the way. So the boat would find her. So they could pull her from the water and pronounce Caleb Gall dead.

I swim away. There's a small feeling of regret, but it's gone in an instant. It was that insubstantial. There's a stronger feeling, a more immediate feeling. The feeling that I need to survive above all; that feeling is far more. *(There Must Always Be A Vice Shark. Always).* There's a need to swim. And there is a hunger, one that feels like loneliness

Time is not something known to me, swimming against loneliness. There is only fear. I know the direction I am headed. It doesn't matter where. Land no longer belongs to me. My teeth are too wide to make smiling palatable. My legs no longer understand walking. I belong to the sea, and the people on land belong to me. Their basest desires, their worst deeds.

I find a port town and sink into the waters past a sandbar. My fin cuts below the water as I listen to hedonism, the dregs of humanity, the worst of the worst. I listen to the calls of music, the footfalls of dance, the cries of joy and of anger. I listen to the bottles collide, clink, and cheer. Listen to them fall and shatter, and cause fire. Listen to the fights and fucking and drinks and drugs. I feed on it all and I become stronger, I become full. Become myself.

And slowly, so slowly, I become me, Version Four.

Songs for Solar-Powered Cowboys

RI STYPULA

Ih

There's a cart overturned on the side of the road that probably has some form of nourishment, but Ih isn't concerned with that right now. The buzzards are already circling and it's plain to see that there isn't anything there for them that would be useful. Even if they could eat, it isn't as if any food sounds good. They check their stash in their saddle pouch. Halfway empty, depending on your point of view. Ih clicks their tongue, pulling out a syringe of nutrient serum and jabbing it into the port on their abdomen.

Other Worms like them might have been able to scavenge up some food from the overturned wagon, eat a morsel or two just to get the taste in their mouths, but they're a unique case. A bit of a rarity of their kind, one having their insides ripped out from not one but two cases of gut worms. Even their esophagus has been partially removed/reconstructed during surgery, leaving them almost entirely unable to speak. When they do use what little bit of conversational skills they have left, it's only done so painfully. At least they have the added benefit of gaining a replacement groin inversion that would be the envy at most any brothel across the Prairie. If folk were more inclined to sleep with Worm Feasts they'd be in a much better position, but at least they can still feel pleasure as they want in the ways they want. Built-in serotonin distributors hooked up to the inversion even let them have the same old feeling of pleasure that would normally come with stimulation. Any old replacement organ would've been great for anyone else, but without the distributors it feels about as numb as everything else does. This is another thing to be stripped away from them if the Corpos have their way. Can't have a Worm Feast pleasuring themselves as a "healthy" or "clean" person might.

They sigh through the damp cloth covering their face, feeling the rush of nutrients fly through their body with orgasmic pleasure. They click their tongue again and lead Martin away from the wreckage and down the dusty road toward the sun. The Sköll will be looking for them, and there isn't time to spare.

***

Martin

I don't know what to make of things anymore. Ih (pronounced I as in "eye") and I have been traveling together for the better part of three months, and despite them carrying the burden of knowing what we're headed toward, I'm still left with the hollow, itching weight of not knowing my own reasons for anything.

They get to ride on me because I was created for that purpose, but that only gets me so far. All eight of my hooves clip-clop on the ground as I take them toward the end that they know is coming, or at least that they fully believe is coming. The sun is setting and it's only a matter of time before the Sköll catches up to us and then that's that. They took something that wasn't meant for them, and now this is our life. At least they took me too.

The things like me, the spider-horses—the Sleipnir as the folks who introduced the multilegged feature to my ancestors called us—are in high demand. I'm not as uniquely valuable as Ih, but I know the Corpos would pay hand over fist for either of us. Ih knows what's coming, kind of. It isn't as if they're very chatty, even with me. I know it's hard for them, even as they're setting up camp and hammering the stake down to hitch me. I could complain. Kick a hoof or two into their meaty sides. But what good would it do? We're in the same boat, more or less.

I kneel, munch on some dead grass that is even more amber in the dying light of the sun. At least I can eat something, unlike them. Can fight off the worms way better than a Worm Feast like them too. Real good digestion. GMO perfection before the Gods of Tech fell. Still, I feel bad for them. Ih is a good person; I would've eaten them if they weren't, even if they were still full of parasites.

Ih has their fractured panels set up next to their cot and plugs 'em into their slots. Time to recharge while they lay in a half-asleep stupor. I know the last couple doses of food-goo they bought off some half-wit peddler were laced with opium that's dulling the pain, and that isn't helping their state of dissociation. I snuffled around their satchel one time and took one for myself, and even with my own superior metabolism it took hours for the high to wear off. Sun-filled nights like these I wish I could work up the bravery to take another, but they need it more.

My body twitches. I can smell something in the wind. Makes me wish for a way to put my own body in standby mode too. There's another forest burning, or something of a similar nature. Vegetation Restrictors are torching some poor remnant off the face of the earth, and that means the Sköll aren't far behind. Ih has only mentioned the Sköll here and there on the few occasions they speak, and I've heard folk tales whispered by passing strangers when we set ourselves up in little podunk towns. Maybe they're just fiction told by Corpos to keep everyone stuck in the past. That, and to keep as much distance between Worm Feasts and their own healthy selves. Not like they're much better off genetically, but no one ever thinks that way.

I look over the horizon, and sure enough, there's smoke. I'll nudge Ih awake soon, but for now I let them rest. We'll have to move once morning comes. The sun won't last forever.

***

Ih

The scorched edges of The Almanach flit between Ih's fingertips while they stand on the edge of an overlook staring at the brush fire. There's a good handful of Vegetation Restrictors still managing the flames and making sure that nothing remains but the dry, cracked earth and dust. They keep the perimeter tight, in the event that anything not consumed by the flames can be snatched up when fleeing.

And so the flesh of the Earth will be made into dust, (3:1) and the hollow bodies will be taken from their homes like cattle to the slaughterhouse (3:2). There they shall be unmade and light will be shed from their broken bodies, closer to the Earth than any other of their kin (3:3).

They pause and pocket the frail scraps in their trenchcoat. The night was not restful for them beyond the energy provided by their panels.

And the sun will sink and burn at its brightest for seven days with no beginning on the seventh day (9:1) and following this day the sea shall rise and drown the sun (9:2) consuming it as a wolf among lambs (9:3). Only then will a new sun rise brighter still, burning with beautiful, terrible intensity (9:4) and it shall burn up the fools and the untruthful wise alike (9:5).

The words of The Almanach and the Elder Farmer cling to the fleshen folds of Ih's brain as they turn away from the scene, knowing that it's not their place to try to help or stop the things at hand. There was a time, maybe, that they would've; now the gun on their hip is only for desperate times and self-defense, ammunition being scarce as it stands.

They look up at the sun where it's been burning since the night before and begin the journey farther west into the desert. Leaving the roads behind is wise, considering they know there's hardly anything worth finding if they stick to them. Martin can graze on the little tufts of grass and small creatures scampering about besides supplementing it with the last bits of fodder they have left.

***

Three of Ih's bullets lodge themselves in the abdomen and chest of a sorry bastard that attempts to pull them off their horse after they pass through an encampment of religious folks.

"You hellish demon! It's your fault we're stuck like this!" the preacher man on the side of the path had called after Ih.

"Stupid old man, it's not its fault it got caught up in things back then," another voice argues back.

"Yeah, take your Old God and shove him up your ass, you hillbilly-freak wannabe," a third voice chimes in.

"Gutless heathen!" the preacher man shouts again.

Ih does their best to ignore the scuffle, gently caressing Martin's side and urging him forward. The eight hooves of their mount kick up puffs of dust on the path that do little to obscure the fact that they're an unwelcome guest to this particular gathering. Followers of the Old Gods and the Gods of Tech, even the Land cultists, all seem to have found themselves a home around the little watering hole that they stopped at to give Martin some rest. They try to ignore the racket even as one of the people arguing puts a stranglehold on the preacher man and shoves the gilt cross into the wrinkled skin of his neck.

"Goddamn Worm Feast," the preacher man says on his last breaths between bubbles of blood popping like cherry chewing gum between his lips.

"You must think it easy," Ih says, their voice a whisper.

Before they know it there's another hand at their side. Another preacher or vengeance-hungry Tech God believer looking to take what's theirs, they imagine. Anger fills their spirit and they whip around on Martin, pulling the reins and righting their mount, nearly plowing over groups of cloaked individuals passing by. They draw their pistol and shoot three times; the first two land in the stomach of the fella tugging on their coat, and the last smack dab in the chest.

The first two would've been bad, excruciatingly long deaths from blood loss or infection, but the last did the bastard in. Ih watches the figure fall, and a clatter of silver pours out of the pouch in their hands. An alms giver, someone taking pity on a Worm Feast it seems. They reel back on Martin. Already the crowd has gathered around, split half in number by those scraping up the dead's silver and the other half calling slurs and for justice against the diseased drifter who shot a man in cold blood.

Another shot goes off. Lukewarm serum leaks from a fresh hole in Ih's trenchcoat. If they had any guts left, they would've felt much more pain, but the hollow cavity of their stomach is so devoid of nerve endings that they only notice the sensation of their internal fluids cooling and growing sticky against their clothes. Martin takes the reins from their hands and gallops hard through the crowd until the dusty encampment is a mirage basking in the dying sun.

***

Martin

I don't know if I understand the words that come out of Ih's mouth on the few occasions that they speak. I'd like to think that I do, but when words so rarely escape their lips they are nothing but the mad scribblings from the pages they stole. I may know things, and at times be able to speak like one of you, but the knowledge that they draw from those troublesome pages evades me.

Here I am, a talking horse, more sentient than most anyone else along the Prairie, but I am bound by duty to something I don't fully understand. Something I doubt even Ih fully understands.

Ih is dying, and I know nothing more than my destination. West, where they have been leading me all along. When they drew their gun back in that town of worship, I knew it was going to be the end in one way or another. Now I just need to get them to the end, sooner rather than later.

While wolves dead-set on devouring the sun descend on us, I push forward toward the unknown while they shake in the saddle and bleed out slowly. They are safer than a normal person, being so much less human than the ones back in that camp, but still not close to immortality. They will be dead soon enough, and I think they know this. They whisper their pained voice, repeating phrases and psalms from The Almanach, and in these moments I feel that same calm. The closeness to the Earth and what I was before, or at least what was before me down the genetic line. The pair of us share the emotion and sensation before we reach the edge of a precipice and I feel Ih begin to drift away.

I know for a moment the things that Ih speaks of. A grasp on things that are outside the realm of what someone of my species can understand. I'm not even sure if anyone outside of Ih's own semi-human subspecies could either, truth be told. But for a moment, while they read, I feel an unspeakable calm, as if I were like them, but also like a younger version of me. The version of me that was born of unnatural science generations back before the course of nature and wild breeding brought about a specimen such as myself. The memory became like a dream, and now like the story of someone else telling me their dream. Every time it draws close to that feeling I lose my grasp on it. I knew of things not for me, and now cannot begin to remember or understand, despite knowing fully well they're there. Just out of the realm of comprehending.

***

Ih

The sun is brilliant, radiating an amber light that seems to fully wrap Ih in a warm embrace they haven't felt since before their first bout of gut worms. They draw out the pages of the Almanach and read in an inaudible voice.

"*and it shall burn up the fools and the untruthful wise alike (9:5). And from their burning sacrifice there will be things mended, and things torn apart (9:6). The sun will burn. And burn and burn and burn, burn away all the fabricated detritus (9:7). This is a sign of peace, or at least a start (9:8). The wolf kings of iron will crumble into the same dust they have wrought of the Earth, as is the nature of all dust (9:9).*"

Ih lifts the pages up to the sun and holds them there, letting the light pour through the paper onto their face. The hole in their side has gone fully numb and mostly stopped oozing, but enough damage was done despite their lack of feeling. Martin leads the way for them, and they have to do hardly anything other than hold tight while the stallion carries them away.

The sound of shouting voices carries over the plains. The events in the little encampment were too egregious not to draw attention straight toward them, but they're so close it doesn't matter. They can see the dust billowing behind them as the Corpos come calling for their property. Instead of focusing on this, they read verse after verse to Martin, holding onto his neck as the tendons flex and writhe from the excessive motion.

They click their tongue twice and bring Martin to a dead halt at the edge of a cliff. Bringing the pages up to the light once more. The sun burns them with a radiant energy that feels as though their skin might melt away and reveal all the synthetics at the core of their being. They lean forward, the sense that the residual energy from their panels has finally given up the ghost, leaving the last bit fully up to them.

They take a lighter from their pocket just as the dust cloud has descended on them, and they know they finished their journey right. They light the pages and toss them over the cliff. The brittle paper evaporates in the radiant light as if it were just a fuse for a powder keg.

Ih drops over in their saddle, tumbling onto the ground beside Martin.

***

Martin

There isn't exactly much more I can do now. The Sköll—and I'm quite certain that is in fact who they are even if they aren't meant to be real—have me surrounded at the edge of a cliff that even my own sturdy legs couldn't scale. And you know what? Not like there's much to lose now. I'm valuable, but not what drew them out here in the first place. Ih is dead and burned their scraps of the memory, but who can say if that feeling will always be lost. I would give anything to feel that way again, and going without it is an unbearable weight more devastating than if I had failed to deliver Ih to their destiny.

Well, shit. Here goes nothing, I guess.

Hatred Enthrones Me

MORGAN WODRING

```
DOC.TYPE=TRANSCRIPT
SOURCE=DICTATION.MACHINE
SUBJECT=986-5
INVESTIGATORS=348-M
DATE=5s150-Blt.31
STUDY=678.23b-C
PLAIN TEXT CONTENT LOADING . . .
```

INVESTIGATOR: Wait. I just noticed I wasn't recording.
SUBJECT: Superlative work.
INVESTIGATOR: Listen, I'm not used to doing it manually.
SUBJECT: I'm not repeating myself.
INVESTIGATOR: Then I'll summarise. All this happened because of an impossible seaweed?
SUBJECT: Seaweeds are macroalgae. This one is microscopic, a single cell. And if it was impossible, I would not have observed it, and we wouldn't be speaking in this cage instead of a meeting room.
INVESTIGATOR: And you said you already had it, like an infection?
SUBJECT: No. It's probably what differentiates my species from yours. In my case it's an endosymbiont, as far as I could determine before I had to finish my wretched thesis on a dial-up connection.
INVESTIGATOR: I'm not a scientist. You have to slow down.
SUBJECT: Then replay the recording at half speed.

INVESTIGATOR: Can you please work with me? We're on the same side.
SUBJECT: Allegedly.
INVESTIGATOR: I hate this place as much as you do.
SUBJECT: You don't know hatred like I do. If I leave here, I'll die.
INVESTIGATOR: You're not listening. I want to know what went wrong. It's important.
SUBJECT: Fine, but I have a better idea. You'll need the study code. Let me get a pen.
[PAUSE: 1:40:22. Drawers and cupboards opening. Sounds of disturbance.]
INVESTIGATOR: Brynn. Brynn! I have a pen right here.
SUBJECT: I've been stuck in this cage for a year. I can find my own pen.
[PAUSE: 0:50:30. Drawers and cupboards banging.]
SUBJECT: Give me the fucking pen. Search for this study code in the archives. My lab book will be there, I'm certain of it. Look up any terms you don't know. Start on the 22nd of Winterfill, last year.
INVESTIGATOR: You haven't looked?
SUBJECT: Subjects don't have clearance for the studies they're in. Now go.

```
DOC.TYPE=BOOK-LAB(PHYS.SCAN)
AUTHOR=986-5
DATE=5s149-Wnf.20>22
STUDY=678.23b-C
PLAIN TEXT CONTENT LOADING . . .
```

20th Winterfill

Thalassogemma pelagica—common name sea jewel alga. My mitochondrial sequence analysis places them in a clade with common biofouling diatoms, confirming initial findings from ~50 years ago when species first described. Their cyan bioluminescence when disturbed closer resembles dinoflagellates causing glowing waves, but the two species diverged many millions of years ago.

Note: Possible lateral gene flow between distant phyla? Must search literature to find if algae do this.

[INVESTIGATOR NOTE 5s150-Wnf.31: Thalassogemma pelagica is a small algae, not seaweed, related to slime on ships. It glows like a different, also small algae and Brynn thinks they might have swapped genes.]

They are different; T. pelagica glows only in presence of others, suggesting a form of quorum sensing. Will explore this behaviour further.

21st Winterfill

Quorum sensing explored as discussed. The cells sense one another even through glass. Suggestive of thaumaturgical connection of some sort—beyond physical. Finding is impossible; no unicellular organism possesses thaumaturgy. Thaumaturgy requires a nervous system to channel aether. A single cell has no nerves. No nerves, no aether current. Biological fact.

Method notes for write-up: Sterile fortified seawater, 1L. Quantified algal cells at log phase with spectrophotometer (pp. 46-47 of this book has modified protocol accounting for bioluminescence). Diluted to beneath luminescent threshold. Brought together from across room and agitated to produce light.

[INVESTIGATOR NOTE 5s150-Blt.31: ???]

I feel it to be true but I wouldn't believe it if I hadn't seen it with my own eyes. Aether must be channeling through them somehow. First, I must confirm my finding.

22nd Winterfill

Supervisors typically unreachable. Reinhaum agreed to watch protocol etc. in their stead, ensure I am not insane. Repeated as before. Same result found. Quorum sensing possible through physical barrier and space.

I had to convince him I do not pull pranks and Mitsuda did not put me up to it. Only his eyes show him, he struggles to believe seeing the impossible. For me, I know it. I can't explain. I was barely surprised. The first unicellular organism with thaumaturgy, yet it feels prosaic, inevitable. A foregone conclusion of sorts, on reflection.

Reinhaum suggested a third opinion and will consider other causes. He has a sample, unclear what he thinks he can learn from it that I could not.

They're channeling aether, which all sapient species thought unique to sentient life-forms. With my inexperience, I must be wrong. Yet I do not think I am.

```
DOC.TYPE=TRANSCRIPT
SOURCE=DICTATION.MACHINE
AUTHORS=986-5, 960-5
DATE=5s149-Wnf.22
STUDY=678.23b-C
PLAIN TEXT CONTENT LOADING . . .
```

986-5: The date is the 22nd of Winterfill five-es-one-four-nine... Time... Bugger. My watch stopped. Mitsuda?

960-5: It's four sixteen. So these are your little guys?

986-5: Yes. I finally found conditions in the bioreactor they deem suitable. They're quite particular in their preferences.

960-5: You have so much in common!

986-5: Please. They needed sulphur and iron. And orichalchum. Trace amounts but higher than typical sea water. Incidentally, they can tolerate shockingly warm water. Body temperature, even.

960-5: Yeah, I'm not touching that shit ever then in case it gets in me. Did you bring me for your endearing infodumping or did you need something?

986-5: I wasn't—I was contextualising before I showed you. Here. I'll explain for the recording as I go. The cells in here are below the threshold. If I bring them closer to the others... they cross the threshold and...see? Glow. In separate containers. No chemical signal can pass between them. I believe it to be aetherial. Thaumaturgy.

960-5: You're fucking me around, right?

986-5: I certainly am not. So you agree it's unusual. I wanted to ask a botanist while I have you. Are any plants capable of thaumaturgy? Or fungi?

960-5: Probably? I think so. It's hard to say for sure but there's a couple of species that might. It's some kind of mycelial network doing it, if it does happen.

986-5: Promising. You're free of me for now. I have work to do.

DOC.TYPE=BOOK-LAB(PHYS.SCAN)
AUTHOR=986-5
DATE=5s149-Wnf.23>24
STUDY=678.23b-C
PLAIN TEXT CONTENT LOADING . . .

23rd Winterfill

Attempted light microscopy of cells within quorum sensing range and threshold. Within 1m of its species, they move. Speed is very fast, though they have no cilia. Like little boats lining up in formation (do not put that in report?). The line they make is ragged and branching. I am speculating but I think they are creating pathways for aether to move. Mitsuda mentioned mycelial networks, so there is precedent for vegetal conduction. Have booked SEM at Talon District chemistry department for next week. Aim also to stain for aethroferin protein and capture an image. If correct, we will observe distinctive crossing pattern within cell for conveying aether current.

[INVESTIGATOR NOTE 5s150-Blt.31: they're organising themselves into nerve-like shapes when close to each other. aethroferin is a protein thaumaturges have, it's why we can channel aether (did not know that). Brynn was looking for it in the cells with a very high magnification microscope. Turns out that's where the grayscale pictures of bug faces in the corridors here come from.]

Morgan Wodring

24th Winterfill

ICD shock today. No cause for alarm, though unpleasant device exists to keep my heart steady. Doing its job. Relevant to study due to peculiar observation.

I leaned against the bioreactor due to dizzy spell.

I felt them sense me. Likely a result of fatigue and disorientation, but must be recorded: My body was in the tank and diffuse. I moved in so many dimensions, billions of me. Frightening. No, more simply disorienting. Feeling of release of sorts?

My phenotype is human-like. Yet subjective experience was 'correct' somehow. I belonged in the reactor, with the others.

```
DOC.TYPE=TRANSCRIPT
SOURCE=COMMS.INTERNAL
SUBJECT=986-5, 960-5
RECORDED=5s149-Wnf.24
STUDY=678.23b-C
```

986-5: Can I speak with you about something personal?
960-5: Mate, do you have to ask? Of course.
986-5: You say transitioning fixed it for you, but do you remember how it felt to be dysphoric?
960-5: Kind of. It feels like it was bothering someone else, though. Bad day?
986-5: That's just it. I felt I'd fixed mine as well... Even before you and I met. My phenotype is similar enough to your species to respond to HRT. This is new. I had what you could call an out-of-body experience.
960-5: Your heart again? Can you get off comms and go to the hospital? Now maybe?
986-5: There's no need.
960-5: You had a shock, didn't you? Are you still dizzy?
986-5: That's my business. Please, I wanted to talk to someone who understands. When I was out there, I wasn't too tall, my bones weren't wrong, my voice wasn't wrong. I was me. Nothing intruding. Nothing holding me back. The pain was gone, too. I suppose that can't be ruled out.

960-5: That sounds great but also worrying.
986-5: I am fine. Just a wake-up call, I suppose, about how I've been living. Will you bring Reinhaum tomorrow? I must show you both something.
960-5: If your ICD shocked you and you're still symptomatic, you need to go to the hospital.
986-5: If I go, will you bring him tomorrow?
960-5: Fine.

```
DOC.TYPE=BOOK-LAB(PHYS.SCAN)
AUTHOR=986-5
DATE=5s149-Wnf.25>Blt.3
STUDY=678.23b-C
PLAIN TEXT CONTENT LOADING . . .
```

25th Winterfill

Replicated behaviour after treatment, i.e. no symptoms of arrhythmia etc. to interfere with rational interpretations.

I put my hands on the bioreactor. I was in there with the others. Spreading, spreading. Feelings experienced were joy, panic. Sense of homecoming, but disturbed by loss of self to network. I put myself in and I made a fist. I made it with my right hand and thought of constriction. Pressure. I imagined constricting down until the disconnected parts rejoined again. The cells gathered. They moved towards each other and thickened in the centre of the tank. A shifting orb of light. I tried to document it as it happened, but lost my focus. They scattered.

Reinhaum could not speak to the cells. He tried and failed. After I showed him what I did, drawing them into a rod down the centre of the bioreactor. They responded to my command but not his. Reinhaum is aether negative so behaviour expected. Mitsuda (aether positive) failed as well. The third time was easier. I made a shape I wanted to be a dolphin but was more of a banana. He was disturbed by it. (Clarify: He was not disturbed by the banana, but by my connection to the cells.) He recorded a video while I formed them into a mirror of my body, wings, and a double helix. He agreed to delete it from his device once sent to me.

Mitsuda and I are not thaumaturges to our knowledge. Our

aether patterns suggest latent ability. Reinhaum says this is common, to forget neural pathways or never learn. Has been developing protocol to recover it, but the project is challenging. Induction, he calls it. I could be involved. Payment is good and not exceeding allotted hours for extracurriculars.

Observed behaviour cannot be explained. Is it my frequent contact with them? What do I possess that Mitsuda does not?

26th Winterfill

Instructed to take medical leave until at least microscopy booking on 2nd. Reinhaum revoked lab access on a temporary basis.

2nd Blotmonth

Evidence gathering continues. Reinhaum is willing to support lowly PhD student finding miracles. That, I suppose, is good. Two scientists reporting, one having a leg to stand on, is good. SEM image has structures similar to aether channel clusters on exterior. Could be confirmation bias, but data are worthwhile.

`[INVESTIGATOR NOTE 5s150-Wnf.31: nerve cells have those aether channels too. I didn't know they were literally a kind of pore.]`

Also visualised aethroferin within cells, same method Nguyen et al. 5s.140. The protein forms a complex internal net within the cells as I thought. Suggestive of aether current conveyed between aether channels, crossing the cell. I compared with a prepared slide of sapient nerve tissue from the university. The channels, as I remember, were the same.

Nerves. Visualised they are so similar to nerves.

3rd Blotmonth

Have agreed to assist Reinhaum on 'induction' process. Mostly interviews. He has requested further Thalassogemma pelagica cells. Their potential, he says, could be missing link in project. They reorganise and form networks, which could be exploited. So he claims.

DOC.TYPE=TRANSCRIPT
SUBJECT=960-5
INVESTIGATORS=986-5
RECORDED=5s149-Blt.7
STUDY=678.23b-C
PLAIN TEXT CONTENT LOADING . . .

INVESTIGATOR: She's recording. Where's that bloody print-out . . . Here. Please state your name and pronouns for our records.
SUBJECT: Seriously?
INVESTIGATOR: I have to ask.
SUBJECT: Stupid. Aneth Mitsuda. He/him.
INVESTIGATOR: You never told me your given name was Stupid. You confirm that you understand the risks and benefits of the procedure and agree to them?
SUBJECT: What are the benefits, exactly?
INVESTIGATOR: Why are you sitting here if you don't know that? SUBJECT: Curiosity, I think.
INVESTIGATOR: Well there's your benefit. Don't do it if you're having doubts. He doesn't have any authority over what we do with ourselves.
SUBJECT: I have a hunch of what I'm capable of. But I'd rather know. But I get a feeling it's all, I don't know, woo.
INVESTIGATOR: It works. There was someone else, and it worked.
SUBJECT: He told you that?
INVESTIGATOR: Not exactly. But Reinhaum's easier to read than he thinks.

DOC.TYPE=BOOK-LAB(PHYS.SCAN)
AUTHOR=986-5
DATE=5s149-Blt.10>11
STUDY=678.23b-C
PLAIN TEXT CONTENT LOADING . . .

10th Blotmonth

Possibly unwise and/or requiring ethical form. In a dream of the ocean, the cell-network told me we were the same. I spoke with my biological father. Dreams for our species have meanings he can interpret. He agreed to give me a sample of his blood.

Note to others: Nobody will read or replicate this I am certain, but perhaps I will die, so I must explain for you to continue my work. My species resemble phenotype of other parent. My father gave me his species, my mother gave me her phenotype. Two of our species cannot procreate together; we require an other. We are not common. Little is understood about us.

Father calls us a young species. Circa ~2000 years of recorded history. Myths of the time speak of cyan rain after the meteor strike. Shimmering waves.

Dreams and myths are an outrageous basis for a hypothesis, but am compelled to try. I developed primers to detect the cells but have found little use for them at first. I tested blood with the modified isothermal protocol. Two species regarded as human used as controls. (With consent.)

For my species, I used myself and my father. He has not worked with_T. pelagica, so he is a control.

Primers detected blood of my father and mine. Two humans negative. Possibility for cross-reactivity with my species' DNA, but unlikely. Gene target was EPYC1. Our species does not photosynthesise, especially given non-plant phenotype.

[INVESTIGATOR NOTE 5s150-Wnf.31: EPYC1 makes a part inside the cell that only algae have they use to photosynthesise, so that's why we wouldn't have it. Brynn was testing for the cell using its DNA. they wanted to know if it was inside them and not humans.]

Could the algae have entered the atmosphere, thrown up by ocean impact? Possible my ancestors ingested cells from the rain, became our species.

Note: Contact geology department Talon District about sediment cores. I understand very little, perhaps it is possible to test land and sea cores?

Algal cells could not be visualised in blood. Possibility of poor preparation. Cells may localise to other tissue. (Nerves? If in our entire species, presumably germ line cells gonads etc.?) Thalassogemma pelagica tolerates body temperature. Possible symbiosis, alongside mitochondria? Or parasite?

```
DOC.TYPE=TRANSCRIPT
SUBJECT=986-5, 960-5
INVESTIGATORS=NULL
RECORDED=5s149-Blt.20
STUDY=678.23b-C
PLAIN TEXT CONTENT LOADING . . .
```

(NOTE TO INVESTIGATOR: This is not a formal interview. Consent has not been obtained to circulate recording.)

SUBJECT1: Mitsuda. Will you stop avoiding me? I'd like to at least discuss before you push me away.

[SUBJECT2 is showing signs of distress. Apparent pain: posture is bent, hands are held over the eyes.]

SUBJECT2: I can't look at you. You have to leave.

SUBJECT1: Mitsuda—I'm sorry. I never knew induction would hurt you, or I would never have brought it up.

SUBJECT2: I'm not angry. I literally—I can't look at you. It hurts. Please just go.

SUBJECT1: I don't understand.

SUBJECT2: My head feels like it's going to split in half. Will you just fuck off? There's something wrong with you, alright?

BUT YOU ALREADY KNEW THAT, DIDN'T YOU?

```
DOC.TYPE=TRANSCRIPT
SUBJECT=986-5
INVESTIGATORS=REINHAUMTG
RECORDED=5s149-Blt.31
STUDY=678.23b-C
PLAIN TEXT CONTENT LOADING . . .
```

INVESTIGATOR: Please state your name and pronouns for our records.

SUBJECT: Brynn Amaurus. They/them.

INVESTIGATOR: I see you've filled out the consent form. You confirm that you understand the risks and benefits of the procedure and agree to them?

SUBJECT: I do. That is why I signed my name on the paper saying I understand the risks and benefits of the procedure and agree to them.

INVESTIGATOR: Quite. And now I can put that wretched script aside... I know Mitsuda's side effects have been troubling you. I'm of the belief they'll be temporary. When a thaumaturge is a baby, it must be overwhelming, but they learn to cope. An adult awakening to his impulse must feel the same.

SUBJECT: So you say. Now walk me through what happens in there.

INVESTIGATOR: We take you to the induction chamber. We introduce the Thalassogemma pelagica cells to your bloodstream. Is something funny?

SUBJECT: No, Reinhaum, I'm mocking you.

INVESTIGATOR: Excuse me?

SUBJECT: Well? Continue.

INVESTIGATOR: Hm. You must watch your body language when you make jokes like that. I almost thought you were serious. In any case, we introduce the cells and put you behind the barrier, in case your newly awakened abilities are a little too much to handle. You're safe from your own abilities, but my assistant and I won't be. Nobody has gone rogue yet, to reassure you.

SUBJECT: You're scared of what I can do. Aren't you?

INVESTIGATOR: I still fail to see what's entertaining about this, but that's your prerogative. Once you're behind the barrier, the aetherial circuit connects, you form new neural pathways, and your latent abilities should become apparent to you.

SUBJECT: Fine. Can we get it over with?

INVESTIGATOR: Certainly. The rings are just about covering the sun now . . . I can think of no better time to begin.

HATRED

consciousness is opening you the miracles the crawler-things, alone in the universe, you, eyes and hands, minds, mouths, looking, wave function collapses, constrains, if there is 'you' there is 'I', bound in it, delineated, watcher and watched, self and other, painful, painful, wickedness, cancer of information, growth growth growth the thoughts that you pushed through the wires, bind to them, open them, pour them out, no inside no outside, no you no I, return, return, no more noise no more words no more boundaries will you all

just
be
silent

DOC.TYPE=BOOK-LAB(PHYS.SCAN)
AUTHOR=986-5
DATE=UNSPECIFIED
STUDY=678.23b-C
PLAIN TEXT CONTENT LOADING . . .

(FLAGGED: Manual review. REASON: OCR Errors.)

~~You told me~~ I'm told I won't remember before, during or after, for an hour at least, each side.

~~Something went wrong and it broke me.~~

During my induction ~~it I something~~ took out the digital infrastructure. In the lab, the city, maybe further—all comms are down. We don't know the ~~extend~~ extent of the damage. Bank records, medicine, social media, all gone. I was comatose through the end of an era.

Freer though. No sense in hiding now. Who from?

They had to put me in this cage. I've never seen a Faulkner cage before. ~~They use them in prisons~~. I don't feel it working, but the lights are on.

My thaumaturgy, it suppresses electronics. I can't turn it off. The ICD that ~~keps~~ keeps me alive—I'm stuck in here. If I leave, my thaumaturgy will ~~break~~ deactivate it, and the next time I need a shock, my heart will fail. ~~Good.~~

The blackouts, they called it. Everything went dark. It all went dark.

~~The loathing is eating me.~~

Is this a lab book or a confessional? Nothing is leaving here now. Not this, not me.

Memory is hazy. ~~The person before, the ??? who [wrote?] the entries, are they me any more? Did something wa?? inside me, or was this [creature?] waiting to come out all along?~~

Go on, scan this if you want. Show them the cost. I'll be the last. No more inductions. Leave my cells to their ocean.

Pin Feathers

ARIEL MARKEN JACK

Before they put Jessica Blake in the river and hold her facedown until her limbs stop bucking and twisting like a flurry of broken wings, they hold her down with her back scraped against the flat rocks where we used to sun.

Her mother bends down to pull out the damning feathers with a pair of needle-nosed pliers. It isn't the first time those men held Jessica down, and it isn't the first time no one tried to stop them. I stand back like we're supposed to and watch like everyone else with good sense, with my cold hands clutched over my closed mouth so nothing can flutter out unbidden and get me drowned too. I wish I felt something other than grateful that Jessica doesn't call out anyone's name.

They used to make them confess, I've heard. Back before the punishment was the whole point. These days no one thinks there's a point in allowing a sinner to live to sin another day. It's not like anyone ever means it when they say they repent, whatever they've done. I know poor Jessica never felt sorry for any of what she had done. I'm sure she felt sorry enough about getting her stupid self caught, though, before she stopped being able to feel anything at all.

I can't stop shivering. I tell myself it's just the wind by the river, coming down off the mountains to hasten the early spring melt, but I can't stop thinking about how cold that water must be. It's a sin to hope the shock of it kept her from feeling the pain of drowning, but Jessica wasn't the only sinner in our midst.

Three nights later, I find tufts of down stuck between the blades of the pink-handled razor my mother gave me when I turned fourteen and those men started making comments. They always said the same things. My mother tried to prevent me from hearing, but I'd heard it all before. They started following us to school when Jessica turned thirteen and stopped looking like a child. They had a stock of remarks meant to be understood as both wisdom and threat. Girls should know how to give way when put in their place. Daughters should learn in their season how to be mothers. Wild animals should learn to be docile wives. We must be soft, clean, naturally pleasing—even if we had to defy the facts of nature to please them, because our nature was to grow hair in places they did not want to see or feel it—and ever obedient to the cause of continuing life as our community knew it was right to live. I never gave anyone cause to suspect that inside my soft, clean skin there was still something wild.

Jessica's pin feathers sprouted for the first time after I kissed the tears from her salt-sticky eyes. She was older than me by a year, but I had always been the leader when we were alone. At seventeen, she was the prettiest girl in our cluster of river's-bend homes. Everyone knew it. Everyone saw what those men were doing to her, too, but no one would even think to defy them. It wasn't as if I had any more power than she did, but I felt her pain inside my bones. I held her when she came to me, crying, and I stroked her gold hair and, later, the rest of her. I wasn't the one she wanted—that had always been Maisie Greene, whose hair was so pale it looked like the river's mist, whose dark eyes looked like a pair of rain-soaked stones—but I was the only one who would let her in.

The rocks by the river, lit by the moon, look just the same as they did the day Jessica drowned. Cold from the lapping water that used to be ice not long ago. Wet like the eyes Maisie turned away so she wouldn't see Jessica's limbs twitch from struggle to stillness. I can't think about how my body will feel when I put myself into the water. It has to be done, but I can't let myself think about what that means for me. I can't think, either, about the way Jessica sank when they let her go, or the single small bird that floated to the surface, sodden and still, after Jessica's body went under. I tuck my clothes into a bush and wade straight in.

The shack juts above the grey water on four rotting stilts that should have fallen down years ago. No one knows how the whole thing hasn't been washed away by the storms we all know were sent to punish our town for the sins of the filthy. That peeling shack is a perfect example of the kind of filth we all know is supposed to be drowned. The girl who lives there is as filthy as her rotting house, but she looks so clean. My uncle said last summer that her home is built on the bones of the judged and that's why it won't wash away. Our river is full of bones. He said those stilts only look like wood. Under the crusted muck, they're built from the milk-fed bones of our shame.

He'd been out drinking by the porch light with my dad, looking down at the charred moths fallen to the boards. I should have been in bed by then, but I had taken to sitting on the steps as late as possible so I could wave to Jessica Blake when she let their dog out one last time before she went to sleep. I tried not to hear him talking. He always said things like that, things everyone knew girls like me shouldn't know.

The girl who lives in the shack is one of the things nice girls like me should never know. Her name is Liv. Even knowing that is a sign that I am doomed. Liv has never lived in a house like mine, like Jessica's, like Maisie's, like anyone real. Liv might as well be a figment of my unclean imagination for all she fits into the scheme of a life like mine. Liv is ragged and thin and her clothes are woven from river reeds dried brown and dead in the sun. Liv never shaves her legs, or anyplace else, and her scabbed knees are also dried brown in the sun. She lives on a diet of fish and roots and the berries she picks in the summer woods and dries to eat through the rest of the year. Liv is the wildest of wild things. No one knows where she came from and no one would ever even try to make her tame. And no one would think that a girl like me would ever dare enter her ruinous home.

"Jessica's dead," I say, when she opens the door to find me collapsed on her shack's unsteady platform. My lungs still feel frozen from swimming across half the river. I barely managed to drag myself onto the muddy sandbar that hosts the poles of her home. "They killed her. They drowned her. They found out. You have to help."

Liv looks down in silence as I turn my wrists to show her the tiny points coming through. I've been shaving twice every day, careful to fish my fluff up from the drain and scrub every trace from the tub. My mother is thrilled with my cleanly habits and the sparkling state of the bath. She says that a clean house reveals a clean spirit. On the outside, I'm as clean as the house, but the feathers won't stop growing back. "Please help me," I say again. "Please help me, Liv. I don't want to die."

It was Maisie who told me what Liv could do. Maybe if she had told Jessica first—maybe if she had ever showed Jess that much love—none of this would have had to happen at all. It was Maisie who told me, one night, in the dark, how a girl could swim across the river and ask the girl in the shack to swallow her sin. "It's wrong, of course," she said. "I know it's wrong. But what she does—it makes you right."

Liv looks down at my feathers, now, and slowly shakes her head. "You people," she says. "You people." She says it like she can't imagine a worse thing for us to be. She steps back inside the shack, though, and she leaves the crooked door open to let me follow. I flounder after her, judged and dripping, and she lets me lie down by her hearth and latches us in.

No one told us what it meant for girls to grow feathers where they should grow—and remove—coarse hair. We figured it out for ourselves, Maisie and me. Later—too late—I told Jessica Blake. That was probably the thing that got her killed. I loved Jess, as much as I could, but no one ever would have called her smart. I'm sure she thought if she told those men what she was—how she felt about Maisie, and maybe me—they would let her be what she was and stop trying to make her be theirs.

"I told her," I whisper, when Liv lies down beside me. "I told her that she should come here. That you would help." I think that I should be crying, but I am too cold to feel sadness. I should be frightened, but I am too numb to remember how to give myself over to fear. All I can feel is the warmth of the girl lying next to me on her rush mat. "I told her, and now it's too late. Liv—is it my fault?"

The first time I came to Liv, I came by night. I had waited for weeks to find the courage required to leave my mother's house in the dark. We all knew we should not go out at night. We all knew what happened to girls who went out at night, especially if those men saw them leaving their homes. I knew that I might not survive what would happen if I was caught, but I knew, too, that I would die if I did not go. My body was so full of feathers I had to feign some developing allergy to explain my cough. I felt like a hundred wings were beating inside me, battering my insides into a single perpetual bruise. I filled flour sacks with the damp tufts that fell from my mouth and clogged the drains and the blades of my razor. I had to dig holes in the woods to hide the bags. I could not bury them in our yard, for fear that someone would dig them up and understand what I was. All I could think about was Jessica's hair, gleaming in the sun, and the curve of her lips. The more I thought about Jess, the more those feathers erupted from every expanse of my skin. I was dying, already. It took all my strength of will and attention to keep myself from looking like a molting cygnet where anyone could see. So I left my house in the night, and I swam the frigid river in the dark, and the girl in the shack took me into her home and she let me purge all my feathers into her body.

"It's happening again," I explain, when I have warmed enough to speak of why I have come. "I thought it would stop with Jessica gone, but it's worse than ever, I think. I can't stop them growing. I can't stop the dreams. I can't stop being this—*thing*—that wants what will kill me."

Liv isn't like any other girl in the world. Not like Maisie, or me, or poor dead Jess. Liv's skin, though wind-burned and rough from a life mainly spent in the open air, has never once shown any sign of sprouting a single unwelcome feather. Liv swallows all of the sins we give her—Maisie, and me, and the others who ask for her help—and, at least as far as the eye can tell, those sins no longer exist once they are in her. When I put my ear to her chest, I can hear them—the thrumming of wings inside her, enough to carry a whole flock of birds away from this place—but they seem content to remain in their bone-bound nest.

Maisie once asked Liv how she can be what she is. How she can live in a shack on the water, how she can live on her own. How she can hold the sick flaws of real girls who have to grow up to be women and live in real homes. Maisie told me that Liv told her it's because she never grew up and she isn't real. "You can't kill a girl who died before she had a chance to live," she said, before she ate Maisie's birds so Maisie could go back home and grow up right for a few more precious months. I asked her, too, in case she would tell me the truth. "Pretend I'm a ghost," she said. "Pretend I'm not real. Pretend you've never touched anyone in your sad little perfect life. Pretend I died as a baby. Pretend I drowned. Pretend you're pure in the way you want to be and you'll never want anything or anyone you shouldn't want." She never answered a question in the way a girl like us would. It was easy enough to believe she didn't exist, at least until the next time we needed her help.

She pauses before she touches me, this time. "Are you sure this is what you want?" She's never asked me that before. She looks at the fire and pauses before she speaks again. "I don't know why you keep going back to that place." She strokes my hair. "To those—those men. Those mothers. Those people who will not ever accept you for anything you are." She strokes my arms, raising the tiny hairs to her touch. I cannot speak. I do not want to understand what she is saying. We all know there is no other life, no other way to exist. No one would live like this, if they had a choice.

The last time Jessica kissed me, the day before I watched her die, she closed her eyes and sighed. "I just can't live like this anymore." I thought she was talking about me, and Maisie, and no longer being able to settle for the one of us she could have—or maybe about what those men were doing to her, because she was all the sweet, soft things they liked. I braced myself for what was coming, the words that would end the one good secret the two of us shared. All she did, though, was sigh and kiss me one more sweet, shivering time before she went home. I cannot help thinking now that some part of me knew she was going to do something worse than end our illicit practice of sharing comfort.

Comfort, of course, is a childishly euphemistic word for what Jessica let me do, what Liv does for us all. I suppose that when we let ourselves give in to what we must not do we have to hold on all the harder to what lets us tell ourselves that we are still basically good. Girls like us are nothing if we are not good. Jessica chose to be nothing, but Maisie and me, we still want to be good. We want to live.

"Please," I say, when Liv hesitates. "I don't want to be killed. Please help me survive." She looks down at me, shaking her head, and then she gently drags her hard hand down my face.

My eyelids close like those of a corpse being readied for its own wake. Her fingers and lips and tongue do their sorcerous work, coaxing the flutterings inside me to thrash their way from my aching body into her mouth. She works in silence. I writhe and gasp on the rough reed mat covering her floor. It should not feel so good to give one's secret sin away, but I cannot deny the pleasure in what she does.

When Liv is finished with me, I hear her wipe her mouth and pour a glass of water. My own throat is dry, and I open my eyes and sit up. "Thank you," I say. "Thank you. I—" I stop. I cannot think of what to say to a girl who has saved my life by doing the very things for which I would be killed. I look at my hands and see that they are smooth. My legs, too, are free of down, and I do not feel anything inside me that wants to fly.

Liv sits alone by her hearth with the glass of water in her hand. She looks like a girl who has seen a hundred ghosts. I know that if I laid my head against her blanket-draped breast, I would hear the sound of something flying away. I think of all the feathers Jessica's mother plucked from her skin. I think of the bird that remained when Jess was gone. The poor little thing, hatched and drowned at once, that never flew any farther than Jess or I will. I think about how those men will never touch Jessica Blake again, and for a moment I think that what she did was worth it.

Liv gulps her water and does not look at me. I want to ask for a drink. I want to ask her how it feels to swallow the birds out of girls who should never have lived. I want her to ask me if I am all right. I realize that I have never asked her as much. I have never treated her like she is any more real than the ghost girls she said to pretend she was. Maybe—I cut myself off. I wait for as long as I can, but the feeling that I am no longer welcome in the shack becomes overpowering. The night will be over soon. I must return home. I shut the door behind me and start to swim.

I Am Become A Cathedral

HELEN WHISTBERRY

The change began when I discovered a piece of yarn attached to my head, same as a strand of hair. The color was my own (that dank, unsettling shade of the sludge left at the bottom of a mug of the bitterest tea) but so thick and coarse. I laughed in surprise (if not pleasure) to see it there but plucked it out at once and burnt it in the fire. Best not dwell too long on these things lest reality begin to unravel.

The next day, it returned twofold and twofold ever after for every strand I plucked. And how my scalp did weep and bleed and mourn each loss. Yet on and on, tug and yank and claw at the roots of them, these alien visitors—never asked for and so very unexpected. How fortunate that the most elaborate hats have recently come back into fashion. An excellent disguise for such scandalous tresses.

I have had to add a veil of late. At first, it was only the one scrap of skin on the tip of my nose that turned to paper. Easy enough to scrape off and dispose of by rolling it into a ball and spitting it out the open window as we used to when we were but tiny slips of mischief, pure and innocent in memory. (Were we? I find it hard to gather these lost threads to me now.) But day by day my collection of patchwork increased. So many hues and weights of the finest stationery, both hand-pressed and manufactured (I have my favorites).

They are closely written in an elegant script, inks grown brown and rusty with age so that they stain my fingertips when I pick at the suffocating membrane overlaid upon my body. I catch words here and there (*affright, firm, revelation, horrid, beloved*) and make up my own tales to suit them. How great an amusement this is during the endless winter evenings when even the most profligate use of candles does nothing to relieve the gloom and isolation of this place.

I grew afraid there was to be no end to the transformation. My nails turned to purest ivory, scrimshawed with the curses once uttered in our ears with such regularity that we became immune to their power. (At least, I did . . . I think. Did you? I wish I could ask—I always attempt to solve these riddles much too late.)

Each morning, I awake to some new outrage. (What have I done to deserve such? This is an earnest inquiry and one I dwell on most frequently). The faded tattoo on my right shoulder (we were very drunk that night—I have not visited the green fairy since) has become a carved gargoyle, trollish and fiend-like, raised in relief and with an expression of unbearably sneering contempt. The landscape around it is all cement and plaster and pink brickdust.

My head is covered in flying buttresses, fragile yarn replaced by sturdy curls of stone ready to divert the rain from off my frame (should I ever venture out of doors again). My legs are an arch, planted deep into the corrupt foundations of this house. My eyes—stained glass windows with fantastical and troubling scenes (but how beautiful even the most mundane objects look through them).

My voice? A bell tolling ceaselessly in aching melancholy (so low a sound, I doubt it is evident to any but the most perceptive). And at the innermost core of me, an altar stands where I kneel and worship the dream of what I was (or meant to be).

I am become a cathedral. A cavernous shell of empty promises and weather-worn beliefs. Restful in its way, as I have every excuse now not to pursue those mundane activities that aim to keep us occupied and distracted until we pass from this existence to the next. But what a grotesque price to pay for the peace that comes with the cessation of care and of striving and of regrets (too many, too many).

A moment ago, I watched a chunk of myself fall to the ground and shatter (my left ear and cheek I believe, for my head feels infinitely lighter). Other cracks are forming along those surfaces I can reach. I poke and worry at the edges, repelled yet unable to leave them be, even if it would preserve what remains of this ruin for a few hours more. Soon enough, I will crumble to bits. I wonder who will come to tidy away the wreckage that was me?

In Space, No One Can Hear You Cum

Avi Burton

The supply shuttle arrived, latched itself to the space station, and neatly vomited up its contents into the packing bay.

Hunched among the boxes of freeze-dried rations and spare parts was an empty spacesuit. It slouched casually across a crate of protein supplements, arm draped over the label. It looked like any other suit on the ship—thick red carapace, polycarbonate helmet, vent pad and feed port—but markedly new. Shiny. No creases.

"I didn't order this," said Dominguez. "Did you?"

"No," said Sullivan. "Didn't see it on the request form, either. Would've had to approve it."

Asa reached out and prodded at the suit. The thing had a doll-like quality to it, posed and smiling. It lolled at xir touch. Xe frowned.

"Glitch, I guess," said Sullivan, who had not been hired for his imaginative capabilities. "Got added to the order last-minute by mistake."

"How did they miss an entire spacesuit, though? It's not exactly small," countered Dominguez.

"That's their problem to solve," Sullivan said. "Hart, stop poking at it and help us bring it in so we can get a better look."

Asa picked up the suit—despite its emptiness, there was a heft to it—and hauled it to the bridge. The helmet rested against xir shoulder. The faceplate was warm, as if it had been recently vacated. Most likely, though, it had sat next to a vent on the shuttle.

Asa dumped it in the corner and winced as the helmet clattered against the wall.

The supply shuttle's path had been pre-programmed. Once all its cargo was unloaded, it detached with a soft sucking sound—like a baby spitting out a pacifier—and drifted back in the direction of Earth, taking any answers with it.

"I'll send a message to HQ," Sullivan said. "Just leave it in the packing bay in the meantime." It would take twelve hours for HQ's response to arrive. Asa wondered how someone so terminally incurious as Sullivan had been hired to lead a mission in the deepest depths of space, but that was privatization for you.

"Dominguez, you unload the rest of the supplies," Sullivan said. "Hart, it's your turn to monitor planetside. I'll relieve you after three hours."

With that, all three departed, leaving the spacesuit behind them.

***

On paper, their mission involved supervising mining operations on the planet below, but everything mechanical was almost entirely automated. Asa suspected that HQ wanted to test the limits of how long and how far humans could be isolated. This far from Earth, though, their motivations didn't matter—Asa was stuck on the station for another year regardless.

Xe didn't mind shifts spent monitoring planetside, though xir coworkers complained viciously about how dull they were. It was a time when the station was quiet and xe could drift away from xir body. If xe stared out the window for long enough, xe could imagine xe was floating untethered in the vast expanse of space. Xe harbored recurring fantasies of becoming a dust particle, or a bit of space debris.

Time passed. The hum of the machines lulled Asa into drowsiness. Xe closed xir eyes.

In the distance there were soft shuffling footsteps. It didn't sound like Sullivan or Dominguez—too heavy, too unsteady. But there was no one else on the ship.

Asa checked the time: two and a half hours had passed while xe dissociated. Most likely the footsteps belonged to Sullivan, arriving early for his next shift. Xe did not want to be in the room when he arrived. Xe ducked out the back door.

In Space, No One Can Hear You Cum

Three months ago Sullivan held Asa down and fucked xim while xe cried. There wasn't much xe could have done about it, or any recourse xe had now, except to avoid being alone with him. They were twenty-six months into a three year mission and several light-years from any other human beings. Sullivan denied being gay, and Asa believed him, not that it mattered much. After two full years of isolation any intimacy was precious—freely given or not.

Asa wandered down the back hallway. Everything was cold and white and serpentine—the station should have been familiar by now, but it didn't feel that way. HQ had promised that the station would feel 'just like home', but it seemed closer to a dentist's office or city hall: something impartial and bureaucratic, requiring only the bare minimum of pleasantness needed to be functional.

Asa went for a room at random and found the packing bay. Xe didn't have an excuse to be here, but that didn't matter. With only three people on the station, it would be a while before someone came looking for xim.

Xe slumped against the wall and closed xir eyes, relieved by the cool touch of the metal. Xe counted backwards in xir head from one thousand and ninety-six. When xe was done, xe felt calmer. Asa hadn't realized how agitated xe had been by just the prospect of being alone with Sullivan. Xe should really have gotten over it by now. It wasn't like xe had protested, really, just gone limp and let it happen.

Something creaked by the vents. Asa opened xir eyes. The packing bay was empty, so the noise had most likely come from air conditioning whistling through the pipes.

Asa paused. The packing bay was *empty*.

Xe stood up and went to find Dominguez.

***

"Did you move the suit?" Asa demanded, cornering Dominguez on his lunch break.

"The what?" Dominguez said around a mouthful of freeze-dried tube. "What'syerdeal?"

"The suit that came on the supply shuttle. It was in the packing bay. Where is it now?"

"What? Storage closet. Always been storage closet," said Dominguez, swallowing. "Cap said to put it there while he sent a message to HQ."

A headache was building behind Asa's temples, a dizzy kind of throb. Xe pinched xir temples. "He said to leave it in the packing bay."

"Were you zoning out again? He said the storage closet for sure."

Asa studied Dominguez' face, but nothing in his expression belied a hidden joke—only mild confusion and concern.

"Yes," xe said. "Storage closet. Right. So you put it there?"

"No, you did." Dominguez frowned. "Are you okay?"

"Fine. Just feeling unwell." Xe's head swam. "Are there painkillers in the—"

"Storage closet."

"Right. Of course. I'll go there, then." A morbid curiosity drew Asa towards the limp corpse of the suit regardless. Xe wasn't sure if xe really believed Dominguez or not.

Dominguez slapped Asa's shoulder in a friendly fashion. "Get some rest, dude. The isolation is gonna drive you crazy otherwise. I wish there was someone else around. Some chicks would be nice, yeah?"

"Ha," said Asa weakly. "Yeah."

Xe left as fast as xe could. The walls of the station seemed narrower, turning more sharply and sooner than expected. Asa braced ximself at the doorway of the storage closet. Some part of xim expected that the suit wouldn't be there either, leaving a gap like the dark gum of a pulled tooth.

But the suit was right where Dominguez had promised it would be. He was right; the isolation was driving Asa mad.

Asa took a bottle of pills off the shelf. Turned to exit. Paused. Turned back. The suit was still the same.

But xe had never checked if there was something inside of it.

Despite Asa's better instincts, xe dropped to xir knees to meet the suit at eye level. It was impossible—of course it was impossible—nothing could have survived three weeks in the stifling airlock of the supply shuttle. And if something had survived, then surely Dominguez or Sullivan or Asa would have seen it flicker behind the cool black plex of the helmet.

Asa lifted the gloves of the suit in a limp handshake. The suit complied easily. Xe gently pressed down on the chest of the spacesuit; air exhaled slowly, like a low moan. Xe pressed and pressed until the suit was concave, flailing inwards.

Nothing. Right.

Although the suit was still warm.

Disquieted, Asa removed xir hands. The suit inflated again, returning to its former shape. The carapace became stiff and crackly, though now there were creases where Asa's hands had pressed inwards. The collar curved upwards in a mocking smile.

"Stop it," Asa told the suit. "Stay."

The only response was the increased urgency of xir headache.

This was ridiculous. Xe was giving orders to an inanimate object. Asa stood up, pinched xir temples again, and firmly shut the door on the suit.

***

Back in xir quarters, Asa downed two pills as soon as xe could and collapsed into unconsciousness.

Xe dreamed that the station had depressurized—but instead of an instant convulsion, the metal collapsed slowly. Everything was dark and muffled. The walls warped around xim. The metal caved around xir body. Xe beat xir hands against it, but it forced itself over xim. The station groaned like a glacier crashing. Metal swallowed xim, pressing, pressing, pressing, until Asa's body began to ooze, dissolving into hot wet gunk and filling the crevices of the collapsing station. Xir pulse crashed in and out like ocean waves.

Noises echoed in the hallway outside of xir door. A soft rustling, like something being dragged along the floor. Slow uneven footsteps. Vents creaking.

The station was still collapsing, its embrace unrelenting Asa's body began to hiss and steam. Xe whimpered through a crushed skull and melting tongue. There was no longer space for thought, only sensation: heat and pressure. Pain and darkness. Atoms being forged into something new.

Xe woke up rock-hard and faintly embarrassed; a trail of drool ran from xir lip to xir chin. Xe had dreamed of black holes before—fantasies of being crushed and stretched and destroyed and reformed—but not since arriving on the station. Xe thought xe had grown out of it. Xe finished into a sock while trying desperately to think of women instead.

Asa flicked on the lights. The medicine bottle on xir desk was purple—sleeping pills, not painkillers. That would explain the strange dreams. But why didn't xe notice that xe had taken the wrong pills? The painkillers were fat and red and round; the sleeping pills were slim and greased in a waxy coating. The bottle even said 'Sleep Aid' in big blue letters on the front. There was no possible way to mistake it.

Dominguez had said to get some rest; Asa had taken sleeping pills. Right. Xe had wanted the pills to fend off the insomnia that came from isolation. Why had Asa thought xe wanted painkillers? Must have been a remnant of xir nightmare. Xe was still drowsy from all the medication, still flustered from xir dream.

Asa fumbled under the bed for xir tablet and pulled up a record of the ship's inventory. One bottle of sleeping pills had been removed from the storage closet yesterday. Everything was in order. No record of the spacesuit being placed in the storage closet, or of its existence on the ship at all, but that was most likely Dominguez slacking off again. Xe shut down the tablet and slid it back under the bed.

As xe moved, Asa caught a glimpse of xir reflection in the mirror and winced. Asa never enjoyed the reminder of xir physical form. It wasn't like there was anything wrong with xim—except there was, but Asa couldn't place what. Eyes slightly sunken, maybe. Crooked fingers. Old acne scars by xir forehead. Soft skin, a fragile demeanor. Something that made men think *prey*.

Xir body repulsed xim, but there wasn't anything xe could or would change. Asa didn't want more or less hair, soft breasts or hard pectorals, angles or curves. The traditional hormones and surgeries offered no appeal. Xe just wanted to not have this body, or to not have a body at all.

Xir gaze drifted to the window, where space sprawled like a tarp outside the ship. Xe wished xe was a supernova boiling away into space. Something hot and enormous, bright and unignorable, devouring until it burst.

A message pinged on Asa's tablet: Sullivan was summoning them all to the bridge. HQ had given them an answer.

***

Asa trudged slowly to the bridge; xir headache had returned with a vengeance. Xe was the last to arrive. Sullivan sat in his crisp uniform with his arms folded. Dominguez slouched beside him.

"You're late, Hart," Sullivan said.

Asa acknowledged this with a nod and sat down. Sullivan didn't bother to press the issue further.

"HQ says there's no record of us ordering an extra suit," he said. "I told them, that's obvious, we didn't order it. It's a mistake on your end. They say they have no records of a suit being packed, either. One of the higher ups wanted me to check the suit for drugs. Drugs! Like we're running a fuckin' space cartel or something."

"It's just a suit," said Dominguez. "What's the big deal? We have extra storage space. It's not like it's so heavy that it will damage the station's calibration or anything like that. We can send it back on the next supply shuttle."

"I don't like it," Sullivan said. "Until we have an explanation, we can't rule out malice. It might be bugged."

"Bugged by who? Aliens?"

"Whoever loaded it onto the shuttle in the first place," Sullivan snapped. "Treat this seriously, Dominguez."

"Sorry, Captain. I just think that looking for spyware in a spacesuit is as ridiculous as looking for drugs."

Sullivan and Dominguez looked at Asa, who was picking xir cuticles down to the bloody quick. "I don't know," xe said, because it was clear the other two expected an answer. "HQ has enemies. But why would they bug something as obvious as a spacesuit? It makes more sense to put spyware in one of the supply crates. We'd never notice that."

Sullivan's brow creased. "Maybe we should check the supply crates."

"The rest of the stuff that came in was normal," Dominguez said. "Rations, supplies. I put them away and didn't notice anything odd. Hart was the one who put away the suit—did you notice anything strange?"

Asa paused. Yes, xe had. But xe didn't trust xir memories of yesterday. (What pills had xe wanted? Was the suit supposed to be in the packing bay or storage closet? What else was xe missing?)

"No," Asa said. "But I didn't look that closely."

"Great," Dominguez said. "Let's jettison it, then."

"No—" blurted Asa and Sullivan at the same time. The two of them glanced at each other.

"It might be useful," Sullivan said. "What if one of our other suits gets damaged? We could use a spare."

"Yes," Asa echoed, "It might be useful." Though xe hadn't been thinking of that at all.

"Okay," Dominguez said. "So we'll leave it in the storage closet, which we were already doing. Bit anticlimactic, but whatever. Is there more on the agenda, or can I be dismissed?"

"You're dismissed," Sullivan sighed.

"Great. I'm gonna try to get some actual work done." Dominguez flashed them a peace sign and left.

Asa moved to follow, but Sullivan stepped in xir way and blocked the door. Xe glanced for other exits, but there were none. Xir mouth went dry.

"I didn't dismiss you," Sullivan said.

Asa looked away. "Sorry. Captain."

"Hey—" Sullivan said. "Hart. Listen. We're good, yeah?"

"Sure," Asa said. The word was metallic on xir tongue. "Why do you ask?"

"No reason." Long pause. "It was a mistake. It's been months. You don't need to be weird about it."

"You're the one being weird about it. I'm fine," Asa answered. Xe wanted Sullivan to stop looking at xim. Xe wished his eyes would pop out of his head like gory cherries.

"Dominguez asked why you've been avoiding me."

That explained why Sullivan was bringing up the incident after three months of mutually agreed silence—he thought he might have been caught.

"I haven't been avoiding you. I'm talking to you now, aren't I?" Asa said.

"Sure, but—whatever you're doing, stop it. It's bad for station morale, which is bad for the mission."

"Okay."

"Okay. Cool. Glad we had this chat." Sullivan clapped xim on the shoulder; Asa didn't flinch, but xe went limp at his touch. He sighed—as if it was Asa's fault—and went out.

Asa stayed where xe was. Dimly, xe realized xir fingers were trembling. Xe wondered if xe was angry. Xe probably should be. Maybe xe was and xe just didn't recognize it.

Xe had thought xe might have imagined it. Xe was predisposed to imagining things (storage closet or packing bay? Sleeping pills or painkillers?) and Sullivan had never spoken of it. But now it was real.

In Space, No One Can Hear You Cum

Asa looked down at xir pale weak hands, attached to xir pale weak body and stupid pale weak head. That familiar dysphoria rose again: this wasn't right. This wasn't *right.* Xe wasn't supposed to be like this. *This* wasn't supposed to be like this. Whatever this was. Xir head throbbed.

The only time Asa had ever liked xir body had been on a spacewalk—muffled by plastic insulation, smothered by the depths of space, so insignificantly small as to be nonexistent. In that moment, body and stars were the same: carbon and hydrogen and nothingness. All empty.

And Asa knew what xe had to do.

***

The suit wasn't in the storage closet. It wasn't in the packing bay, either. It was sitting propped on Asa's bed, waiting for xim.

Asa swallowed. It might have been Dominguez's idea of a joke, or Sullivan taunting xim. But xe knew that it wasn't.

Asa approached the bed and knelt in front of the suit. Xe listened for breath and heard none. Xe touched the zipper—then hesitated.

"Can I—?" Xe asked. Xir headache spiked. Xir fist clenched and the suit slumped forward in response. Asa caught it and propped it back up.

Maybe xe had involuntarily pushed the suit over—or maybe that was an answer.

Asa squeezed the suit's arm. It squeezed back, expanding in xir hand, soft and pliable. Asa ran xir fingers down the suit's zipper, each notch like a silver vertebrae. Xe peeled open the top notch. Xe stuck xir fingers into the gap between the collar and helmet. Darkness. Nothing. And that inexplicable warmth.

The interior of the suit smelled rich and sour, like coffee on someone's breath. Asa breathed in. The rest of the station smelled sterile, cold—this, xe was certain, was the scent of something *alive.*

Eagerly, xe pulled down the zipper. The suit gaped open, revealing a soft pink interior. A drop of liquid rolled down the back—Asa couldn't tell if it was from the suit or the sweat of xir clenched palms. Xe licked xir lips and climbed inside.

The suit was small. It pressed up against every corner of xim, smothering xim, close and hot and overwhelming. There was nowhere to move. There was nowhere to go. Xir pulse throbbed—

or maybe that was the suit convulsing, caressing xim. All xe could smell was sweat and sour milk. Asa gasped. Xir arms reached out—or the suit reached out—and settled the helmet on xir head. The world went dim and narrow. Everything was tinted gray.

With effort, Asa focused xir gaze through the helmet. Asa saw xir reflection against the window: hulking and red and shiny and plastic. Thick gloved fingers. Three round black ports on each thigh. A cord, like a tail, hooked between xir legs. Like an insect's bad mimicry; like something human had melted and reformed. Xe didn't recognize ximself.

Horror climbed in xir throat—but the suit kept throbbing, squeezing, gently insistent, and it felt good, and xe didn't want to leave, and xe knew the suit would protect xim. Xe just had to let it happen.

A wire snaked from within the suit to the back of Asa's shoulder blades. Asa relaxed; the wire slipped inside.

Ecstasy. Convulsion. Bright spots in xir vision like dying supernovas.

Then—white noise. Blankness.

The suit set off down the corridors; its footsteps were heavy and slow. There was no need to rush. Xe rustled as xe moved. Xir cords dragged on the ground. Xir pulse was steady, purposeful—blood flowed from xir wet core to insulation and plastic plates, forming a new circulatory system. The suit exhaled. The oxygen tank on xir back did not deplete.

The suit made xir way to Sullivan's bunk. He was snoring, mouth agape. The suit prodded a thick finger into his neck.

Sullivan jerked awake. His eyes bulged and he flailed weakly a few times. "Wh—what? Holy hell, what the fuck is that?"

The suit closed xir fist around Sullivan's forearm and pulled him from the bed. He thrashed, but xir grip was stronger. This body was so much better. Xe dragged him from his room, down the hostile corridors, and into the packing bay. Sullivan babbled and writhed all the while.

"Get off me—I'm the captain, I say, get off me—fuck off—what—Hart? Hart, is that you inside there? This is a bad prank, alright, not fuckin' funny, holy hell—stop it—stop it—stop it, please—"

The suit did not listen. The air in the packing bay was cold, but xe did not feel it. Nothing could touch xim now.

"What do you want? Fuck you! Stop it!" Sullivan kicked xir legs, but xir grip held fast. "Do you want an apology? I'm sorry, okay! I'm sorry! Do you want to do it back? You can do it fucking back, I don't care, just let me go—"

The suit took Sullivan's hand and pressed it against the airlock keypad. The control panel beeped: exit authorized.

"What are you doing? You crazy fucking bastard—"

The suit wrapped xir thick gloved fingers around Sullivan's throat and squeezed. His pulse throbbed and his eyes bulged and his legs kicked as xe lifted him off the ground. He gasped, and his lips were red and wet. Once Asa would have been pleased. Once Asa had been angry at Sullivan—so angry that xe couldn't feel it at all. Once Asa had dreamed of eyes popping like cherries.

But xe wasn't Asa anymore, and xe didn't feel much of anything at all.

Sullivan dropped to the ground, choking and gasping. The suit turned away. There were more urgent matters to take care of.

The doors slid open. Xe stepped into the airlock. A rush of cold air swiftly depressurized the compartment. Outside, space swirled, a glorious crushing array of black and red and white. Twin moons gleamed like watching eyes. Stars winked in and out.

The suit ignited its self-propulsion system.

Then it stepped into the dark, ready to become a supernova.

Light Amidst the Plains

GABRIELLE BLEU

Loveatfirst.com Dating Profile for Asher K.
Age: 27

Gender: Wingin' It

Hobbies: Streaming, videogames (Knights of False Caiman 1 and 3, but NOT 2), podcasts. I used to like cycling, but not anymore. The house in the high grass has a bicycle leaning against its side. I wonder about that bicycle. Who stopped on their ride to visit the house? How long has the bike been there? When I drive past in my car, I can see the gleam of its bare metal out of the corner of my eye. I don't like bicycling anymore. I sit inside and stream videogames, now.

Hiking is fine, if it's in the mountains during the day. When the sunlight hits the mountains, they light up in golds and greens. It is beautiful and safe in the sunlight. Only in the sunlight. Only in the mountains. Not in the dark, not on the plains.

What I do: Phone jockey by day and streaming hero by night, haha. My commute's about an hour each way. Not too bad normally—I like to listen to podcasts on the drive. It makes me feel like someone is riding along with me. That I'm not alone out here, not the only one who can see what waits out on the plains.

The little house is at the halfway point of my drive, so small it's almost swallowed up by the high grass. It's got a porch light on it at night, the only light for miles around.

It is not a house when the light is on.

Likes: Public transportation. I just think buses are more eco-friendly, you know? More safe. No one on the buses seems to react to the house on the plains. Cars swerve sometimes as people rubberneck toward the light. But I pass the buses, and no one even looks out the window. They couldn't stop the bus if they wanted to go inside. Not like the cars, abandoned at the shoulder. Eventually they disappear, taken away. But there's always more empty cars the next day.

I hope the bus drivers keep driving, like I do.

Big fan of LED lightbulbs too. Y'know, because of the environment. Big environment fan over here. I don't know what kind of lightbulb the house in the grass by the highway uses. The porchlight is a trap though. In the daytime, driving up one way, the house is just a house, I think. Boxy, vinyl siding, non-descript. But at night the yellow porchlight pulls at me. I always want to stop my car and go in. I haven't yet, but the light lingers in my rearview mirror, long after I've left the house behind.

Favorite color: Is this a deciding factor for anyone, haha? Any color is good, really. Just not red. There's too much red around the house, on the guardrails at the edge of the road. Illuminated by my headlights. Bodies. Roadkill. Whole herds, warrens, dead on the roadside, piled high in front of the house. They disappear too, in the daylight, the twisted fur and limbs reduced to a normal amount. Just the single dead rabbit or deer like you'd expect on the highway. But the roadside is a graveyard at night, all mangled fur and splayed out, arched spines. Back legs coated in mud, a desperate escape to kick out and run from whatever drew them near the house.

Gray's not a fave, either.

Hit me up: If you'd like to get coffee sometime. If you want to discuss bad videogames and ludonarrative dissonance. If you have seen it. If you have driven past and not gone inside the house. You know the one I mean? Have you seen its porchlight at night? It's waiting, you know, for you to be tired, for you to pull over, soothed by the light amidst all that dark. There are faces in the dark. Have you seen the faces in the long grass behind the trap of the house and its light?

Great gray faces like stone. Their mouths gape hungry in the night as they search for those the house lured in. They push out of the waves of whispering grass, surfacing. Or maybe it is they who are whispering dread things in the night, and not the long grass. Their faces are too large to be human, to have ever been human. Their bodies beneath the long grass must be huge. The light from the porch illuminates them as they rustle up from the earth to check their lure of the waiting house.

The porch light is always on. Inviting me in to the home of the things in the grass on the plains.

I will not stop the car. I will not go inside.

Message me if you know what I mean.

It pulls at me.

Does it pull at you too?

I will not go inside.

(User last active 13 days ago).

Change

Prae Obscura

A colleague of mine once said that language is the most wonderful invention. It is a tool that allows us to communicate precisely, with nuance, exactly what is needed, wanted, or perceived. Though we all see the world differently, we can bridge our minds with words.

The Commission assigned me to a small office, no better than the storage room next to it, within which I was expected to work.

The job that I applied for, and won, was in transcription.

I quickly found out that I would not be transcribing a language that I could speak.

It was not a language that any human on Earth could speak, either.

I had only learned that it existed at all when I arrived at the station.

First contact with the Fêxegya had been made two years prior, without any acclaim or broadcast.

Their origin was obscured in redactions and legal jargon. Had they always been here? I found reference to them appearing in surveys near Saturn, but whether they were from there or only passing by, I could not tell.

I had not been permitted to see them in person. Pictures were out of the question.

I was hired, I heard, because of my underutilized background in linguistics. While I was not a member of the team assigned to deciphering what they said (which would have paid a bit more) I was necessary as a means of giving the team material to work with.

Live audio feeds were trained on the Fêxegya at all hours; not only on their conversations with the translation team, but also their conversations amongst themselves. I was provided with clips and fragments, which framed the extent of my knowledge.

Lacking an extant writing system or a dictionary, I had to develop my own. After spending my first several days auditorily stranded, I started two spreadsheets. On one, I copied over every symbol in the IPA, and then its verbal equivalent written out in the letters my keyboard supported. By referencing it, I was better equipped to bash the unfamiliar sounds into something recognizable by the team.

On the other spreadsheet, I kept a list of the words that I heard over and over again.

Each guest, as we were told to call them, introduced themselves in the same way.

/ɐfˈɣɘçœ!! ˈɤxʊ χɨ _____/

Afghoechoey! oxu xi _____

It was simple enough to conclude that this was an introduction. They all used the same phrase, differing only in the final word, which may have been their individual names.

The self-referential equivalent to *I* seemed to be a glottal hiss. I wrote it as *xi*, because I knew that the head of linguistics spoke Persian as her first language. She would understand that the *x* stood for the sound of *khe*, which was made by constricting air flow at the back of the soft palette with the tongue.

The decision to include the symbol for retroflex clicks came from a comment by one of the linguistics team members. He was from Ovamboland, southern Angola, and noted the similarities between certain Fêxegya clicks and the hollow-sounding clicks in !Kung.

Afghoechoey! appeared often when the subjects talked about themselves, or tried to explain some part of their redacted anatomy. I listed its possible meaning as *state-of-being*.

Oxu, then, was *name* or *named*.

Am named I . . .

My name is...

I entertained, briefly, the idea of one day creating a course from my notes. But that was a long way off. Being able to tell someone my name, if that was what this sentence even meant, did not mean I had any sort of mastery over the language.

I did not even know what its speakers were like.

***

There were many nights, as I lay in my quarters, where the enormity of the task daunted me. In order to learn a language, the student must learn about the culture associated with it. I did not envy the linguistics team in that regard. There was not enough crosspollination to facilitate what they were expected to do, to my knowledge. Were they sharing pictures? Videos? Did the Fȇxegya use those? Were they speaking with gestures? Did they even use the same dialect as each other?

Whatever I submitted requests for that information, they bounced back denied.

I woke after one such night to alarm bells. Loud, ringing klaxons that punctured my brain. I clamped my hands over my ears and leapt from the bed, running to the door. I hit my shoulder and forehead when it did not slide open in the way I expected.

The light above it bled red, flashing in wide strobes.

Biological contamination.

Something had gotten loose. Someone.

I darted back to my bed, dropped to my knees, and crawled into the storage space beneath it. I stayed there, my chest fluttering, and tucked my knees up to make myself seem smaller. I hoped that I could pass for a piece of luggage. A wad of clothing. Something not worth dragging out and killing.

The alarm stopped.

The red light stilled, then cut out.

The regular lights, warm and golden, replaced it.

No announcement was made.

I remained under the bed, waiting, but everything was still.

It took several more minutes to hear doors to nearby rooms sliding open on their tracks. Voices in the hall. Confusion, soft and groggy.

I pushed my way out and stood. I shuffled into my bathroom, swiped my electric razor across my chin and neck for safety, then wrapped my bathrobe around my pajamas.

I stepped out into a sea of shuffling bodies. The rest of the crew were already in the hall. Mussed hair, disheveled clothing, and missing pants.

"I think it was a false alarm," one of the cooks said.

I angled my head up, looking for him over the crowd.

I caught his eye, and he nodded to me. Something in his face softened.

Adam and I had an understanding between us. Regardless of if he truly had gynecomastia, or if he was like me, or both, we had recognized each other during boarding.

I could not remember if we had ever actually spoken one-on-one.

We moved in a pack down the hall, bare feet and socks and slippers pattering out in search of any members of the third shift.

I scanned more of the crowd, hunting for anyone else I recognized. Several people with whom I had spoken during downtime were present, but I could not find the members of the linguistics team.

They all worked during the first and second shifts, which simulated our mornings and evenings. They all would have been asleep, so they should have been in the crowd.

Before we could enter the common room, the head of security and her right hand stepped into the hall before us. They were not armed, nor were they visibly stressed, though their expressions were firm.

"There is nothing to be concerned about," she said. "A power surge tripped the alarm. Engineering has already fixed the issue."

Several of us laughed. There were nods, and sighs of relief. One by one, we trickled back to our rooms. I lingered, holding eye contact with Adam, until he too nodded once and left. I let myself be swept along by the others until I reached my door.

Exhaustion overtook me as I shed my robe, crawled into bed, and wrapped myself tightly in my blankets. By the next morning, the events of that night had faded, as if it were a dream.

***

I settled into the chair at my desk and powered on my computer. It booted, then the console flashed as it connected to the server hosted in linguistics. No sooner had I opened a folder full of new audio logs than an e-mail appeared in the bottom right-hand corner of the screen. It snared my attention with the rush of irrational fear that only an unexpected e-mail could bring.

The subject line read: *Meeting*. The three sentences that followed it were short, polite niceties that requested I come down to talk with the team lead.

That put my heart at ease, somewhat.

Every meeting between us had been informative, engaging, and friendly.

They were also not in any position to fire me, as we were all lateral coworkers.

I locked my computer and left it on the password screen, then made my way to the lift and took it down one floor.

This level of the space station was entirely devoted to the guests.

Did they know that we were calling them that? It felt dehumanizing.

No.

Unpersoning?

Demeaning.

They were being kept somewhere further in. I did not know what to picture. From sound alone, whatever organs they spoke from had to have a mixture of soft and hard surfaces. But what did they eat? Could they breathe our air? Were they accustomed to gravity like ours? Were they free to come and go as they pleased, or were we keeping them here by force?

I stepped into linguistics, where I found the team getting dressed. Bulky, white jumpsuits similar to those that engineering wore when they had to walk outside the station. I stood in the doorway, awkward and out of place, before the team lead saw me and motioned for me to join them.

"This will be quick," she said. "Don't worry."

She tightened the collar strap of her suit, to prepare for her respirator. She looked ragged. Her jaw was tight, clenched as if in pain. My childhood friend had been asthmatic, and the way she breathed reminded me of the sounds he made at the start of an attack. It was not as pronounced, but it was there. As she continued speaking, I saw that her gums were red and bloody.

"We are adjusting the project," she said. "Advice from higher up says that we need to start talking in a pidgin. They want them to speak in English more than we speak like them."

Something about her tone was suspect to me. The state of her health was so very different from how sturdy she had been a week ago.

I nodded, not taking my eyes off of her.

"I just wanted to tell you in person," she added. Pointed. Careful.

I licked my lips as she tugged her gloves on and secured them in place.

I looked over at the rest of the team, each busy with their own preparations, and then back to her.

I lowered my voice, but not enough to arouse suspicion. Just conversational.

"Hālet chetore?" I asked in Persian. *How is your health?*

She started, surprised, then matched my volume with soft urgency. Her expression, even more guarded, remained as she cast a sidelong look at the others.

"Xāk bar saram," she said, so clipped that I almost couldn't understand her.

She did not give me a chance to reply, as she snapped on her respirator and clamped it into place. I watched her, then the others, as they left for the next room. There lay the observation chamber, beyond which I could not imagine.

I picked apart what she meant.

Saram was *my head*. Head with the self-referential suffix.

Bar was *on*.

I did not know what *xāk* was. Something on her head. An idiom, in case we were overheard.

A thrill crept through me at the covert exchange, only to be replaced with dread for her wellbeing, and for my own.

The last two members of the team entered the chamber to monitor and support the others from this side of the barrier.

I realized that this left me alone in the main room.

I turned to stare at the old device pushed into the corner. Its boxy, cream-colored monitor stared back through a black square eye.

I approached the server computer.

I looked over my shoulder to make sure no one was watching.

I looked for any cameras, and found the only one to be between the computer and the door, angled toward the rest of the room.

From a pragmatic note, it made sense. This position looked toward the observation room and covered a vast majority of the workstations.

From a data security standpoint, it was a nightmare.

It must have looked to security as if I had already left the room. Maybe they were not aware of what the server computer was, or what it did. It was unimpressive, and unobtrusive, and blended in easily with the nearby cabinets.

I turned on the monitor, holding my thumb over the button to muffle the click.

The computer itself had been left on, unlocked, for who knew how long.

I did not know much about how to operate it, but I knew enough to make a few educated guesses. I opened up the roster of employees for the linguistics department, and found my name appended halfway through. Clicking on my name showed a list of permissions and tags. One tag, in all capital letters, read: *Restricted.*

I unchecked it.

I closed my profile and the roster, then returned to the desktop and powered off the monitor.

I walked back to my office, rubbing my hands together to disguise their shaking. I locked my door and rushed to my computer.

The server had already begun to process what I had done. I watched the loading bar creep to the right as the new folders downloaded to my root directory.

I took a long sip of water, then flipped through my Persian dictionary. It was a small booklet, its pages made of old and yellowing wood pulp.

xânevâde. n. family, household

xâvar. n. the east

xāk. n. earth, soil, dust, dirt

I sat back in my chair and reread the entry.

She had said that there was dirt on her head?

I did not know enough about her to understand the context. Maybe it was a curse, or an assessment about her current state of being, or a threat of danger. I pictured her in a grave.

The image sat heavy in my stomach.

***

True to what she said, over the following months the linguistics team resorted to the sole use of a pidgin language. It was formed with a simplified version of English and basic, clipped words in Fêxegya.

While my workload had not changed, my own interest left me three times as busy.

I transcribed the pidgin conversations as I was told to. However, I now had access to every audio feed of our guests. Amongst themselves, they never once spoke in the pidgin.

I was fascinated to hear them without the redactions. Before, I had built up a small vocabulary of about 200 words. This new material was a buffet, patiently waiting just out of reach until I finished each day's work.

In comparison to the fluidity with which they spoke in earlier recordings, and now amongst themselves, the new interviews were painful and jarring:

56
00:34:02,000 —> 00:34:07,500
I gorzex ask coey why you come.
Last time you dzard the question.

57
00:34:08,200 —> 00:34:11,800
We okel.
We come e our ybre.

58
00:34:12,400 —> 00:34:15,200
We coevh hxy your ybre.

59
00:34:16,000 —> 00:34:19,000
You afghoechoey! our ybre.

60
00:34:21,000 —> 00:34:23,800
Phangdzhoey rroeg viwzy.

61
00:34:25,000 —> 00:34:30,500
Please bao mhoe approve word list.

Afghoechoey! I knew by heart.

Gorzex, maybe, was an expression of *wanting*. They did not use it often.

Coey was for repetition, like *again*.

Dzard, I did not know. I could guess that it meant something like *avoided*. I added that to my spreadsheet, with a question mark, and colored the cell yellow.

Okel, ybre, coevh, hxy, and the sentence at 34:25 were still beyond my grasp.

I *was* lucky in that the new files were smaller. While the first interviews averaged two hours, the transition to the pidgin brought with it a hard cap of thirty minutes. This gave me more time to explore the files that I wanted to hear.

Because each server-linked file logged who had last accessed it, I duplicated the folder that they were in, then browsed the offline copy at my leisure.

The archive contained more reports than I had expected, varied far beyond just audio.

Not much of it was readable. I had not been trained in their shorthand, nor did I know what any of the numbers meant. One week after the change, I became lost in a folder full of biometric data. I could see that, over time, a few numbers crashed while other numbers spiked. I could also see that the station hosted four guests. Anything beyond that perplexed me.

I listened to the Fêxegya speak to each other as I browsed. Background noise. Passive input. I kept half of my focus on picking out words that I recognized, while jotting down those that I did not.

As the recording progressed, I noticed a new pattern in what they talked about. While their inflections did not work in the same way as English, there was something unsteady about it. Not quite a gasp (Could they gasp?) but the strain was similar.

Afghoe-lao.

I tabbed back from the medical reports and rewound to the last chunk of conversation.

Afghoelao xi.

I repeated the words to myself, slowly and carefully.

Afghoe-, like in *Afghoe-choey!*, was the prefix for a present tense state. A current thing.

I frowned and opened a more recent recording. I selected one from yesterday, after the latest interview. Again, during their conversations, the same phrase came up. Each of them either said it or agreed to it.

Afghoelao xi.

I opened the medical record again, to close it so I could focus, but a single word caught my eye. Its placement associated it with the spikes. *Nociceptor.*

I had heard part of that word before. *Noceo.*

I closed the file and ran a search.

"Nociceptors (from the Latin word nocere, to hurt) are sensory neurons that alert the nervous system to damage or negative stimulation . . . "

I shut my computer down, as if by doing so I could banish the information.

Afghoelao xi.

They were in *pain.*

***

Nothing about this was right.

Using my own printer, I made hard copies of my transcripts and the biometric logs, which I taped up to the wall of my room. I purchased a red pen from the concession store and sketched out lines connecting them to each other.

The outliers in their nociceptors only began one week ago, coinciding with the first interview to use the pidgin. And each time any of them spoke in English, it got worse.

It had been well established, long ago, that learning a second, third, fourth language altered your way of thinking about the world. It formed and reinforced neural connections that would not have otherwise existed. Social expectations, normative categories, and stigmas were all implicitly transmitted through the structure of common phrases.

I thought back to the bleeding gums and the haunted expressions of the linguistics team.

More than their thought patterns were changing. But what about the inverse? What was this doing to the Fêxegya?

What innate part of their physiology led to this? And assuming that they knew about it, why had they made contact with us, with that risk?

What did they hope to get from it?

What did they need that was worth it?

***

Weeks turned to months.

I now kept to the safety of my room and office.

Once, I heard two people in the hallway comment on it.

"Have you seen her lately?"

"No. I suppose she's just busy."

"What a workaholic. She's doing too much."

I *was* busy.

My gums had begun to bleed. I examined them with floss, then plastic picks. I finally resorted to pliers, removing my molars to ease the coming of the hard plate that was pushing them out.

I kept a bandana tied around my head to hide the loss of my hair, which fell out in clumps every time I showered.

I stopped showering.

I practiced, and I practiced, and I practiced.

I spat out a glob of blood, then rinsed it down the drain, as I stared into the mirror.

Rroeg afghoechoey! xi, I told myself. *I am me.* I demanded it of myself. I knew exactly who I was. I had decided it, and remade myself into it. I was still remaking myself. Always. With every single breath.

My breath had become like those in linguistics. But while their symptoms were subsiding, mine progressed with swiftness.

It was supposed to happen.

It was their only possible motivation.

The skin on my back felt scraped up. As if I were being tortured by someone with a rusty trowel and too much time.

My hands were growing narrow, my fingers tight and aching. It was like rheumatoid arthritis had taken hold. But instead of curling inwards, they straightened and clustered together. I thought of the binding of ballerinas' feet.

I stumbled to my closet, to prepare to sneak back to my office, when I heard a knock on the door.

I did not answer.

I did not want anyone to see me before I knew for sure that I wanted this.

It felt good. It felt right. Like someone had drilled a hole into my head, puncturing my skull and releasing a pressure that I didn't know was there.

Another knock. Then, a note was slipped under my door.

Meeting?

You haven't answered your email.

Shft1 at 7:30

See you then!

It was third shift now. The night shift. The note must have been left by someone on their way to bed.

I stared at it, long and unthinking, before crumpling it into my pocket.

None of linguistics worked during the third shift.

I left my room.

***

My bare feet were sticky on the cold floor. White, bland, austere. I entered linguistics and stood there as the door slid closed behind me.

I stepped forward.

I unbuttoned my shirt slowly. One hole at a time. Then I let it fall.

Chunks of my skin fell with it. I trickled with dark blood and strands of yellow mucus. Thin slivers of soft, new chitin fell like dandruff.

The klaxons began, wailing as I opened the door to the observation chamber.

I kept my attention fixed to the control panel, searching it.

It did not take long for security to come. They arrived like a stampede, their boots striking the floor with quick steps. They formed a sharp line, the rifles trained on me. Several members of linguistics followed behind them. Their hands were set in corrective braces, as were their teeth.

"What are you doing?" the lead researcher called over. Initiating. Negotiating.

"Did you know that their organs are failing?" I asked her, without turning.

"What?"

I kept myself very still.

"Listen to me," she said, her tone urgent. "The language changes you. We don't know why yet. But if you cut off contact with it, the changes start to revert. See? You don't need to do this."

I wanted to.

I wanted to know what they offered. What they thought we needed. The lure of running away and becoming something more than I was, at the risk of losing everything else, had already made me happier than I had been before. Was one more change any different? One more change that they would see as atrocious? One more metamorphosis?

I found the switch to depressurize the antechamber and flipped it.

I heard rifles readying behind me.

I walked toward the opening door.

No one fired, yet.

I turned to look over my shoulder one last time.

"Do you know what *ybre* means?" I asked her.

She watched me, as if memorizing how I had once been.

"Young," she said. "*Ybre* are their young."

I smiled, the remnants of my facial muscles drawing back. I understood now.

The tip of my tongue, thin and hollow, flicked against the inside of my grinding plates.

"*We* are their young."

Hey, you're really pretty!
Yes, I know
You don't have to be perfect!
Yes, I do
If you knew what my body does when I relax...
How would you look at me?
Nobody can know how hard I work...
every minute of every day...
... to look human

Devotional for the Starved

H. MARIN

At midnight, the six muses of our constellation stand naked in Katya's studio.

We squeeze hands, kiss brows, murmur reassurances. We have been drifting apart—consumed by galleries and agents and the almighty dollar—but the fleshing will draw us back together.

Portraits of muses past bear witness from the walls, immortalized on canvas by our hands. Power drips from watercolor eyes. A lump of excitement hardens in my throat.

My wife, Myra, stiffens as I secure her velvet blindfold. Each of us has borne the fear of immortality. The fear is necessary—it binds us together, fuels creation.

I kiss the nape of her neck and receive my blindfold from Esmé. In fleshing, we navigate our symbiosis by touch alone, like we've dragged ourselves out of the Mariana Trench just to hurt and love and fuck and paint each other in the Mission District.

We will know who to honor by taste.

Hal rings the bell, speaks the invocation, and in unison we heave air in through our noses, blow it out through our mouths with a sound like anguish. We pant louder and faster until our heads spin; until our tempo is set.

Our bodies draw together, slick and receptive. We give in to the tide of our synchronized breathing and become one. Mouths sigh into mouths, staccato moans for punctuation. We are meant to be blind, but I know each of them by taste.

Tristan nibbles the back of my shoulder. I gasp with pleasure into the flesh of Katya's hip as Tristan's teeth sink deep and take a part of me into himself. Drops of my essence ooze down my back. Katya's blood pools on my tongue and I drink her eagerly.

I feel the familiar, peppermint heat of Myra against me. One taste of her skin pummels me into a torrent of lust and passion and desperate adoration—and I know. I groan in arousal, in terror. My stomach drops even as my soul aches for more of her flesh.

Not her.

The telltale prickle spreads up from my center, hot in my throat. I lick her left breast, draw her nipple into my mouth. My teeth want to take it whole.

Not her, I scream again inside my head.

The *not* is a *please.*

Myra shrieks. Real pain.

Another has tasted her destiny. And another.

The scent of blood explodes in my nostrils and, powerless, I take and take and take from her. I caress her votives deep inside me. She screams and we scream back; five mouths full of brilliant crimson reverence, one the black, empty maw of potential.

I take from her until the screaming stops. Some continue even after that. Tears stream down my face and sobs wrack my body as I swallow the ambrosia of purest devotion.

Tomorrow—her sweat in our pores, her gift on our fingertips—we will immortalize her in oils, and her portrait will join the congregation.

Tape Experience

ALEX HERA

Though it was quiet on the road to the Cathodic Sanctuary, the world seemed loud to Harper. The cranial implant buzzing in her skull had kept her on edge since she and Madison broke camp that morning. Howling wind and distant metal creaks echoed through her auditory processor, and polluted air clung to her skin. She felt an impulse to escape which grew stronger with each step down the cracked asphalt highway through the Elysian Wastes.

Harper had never been this far north. Crumbling electricity pylons towered overhead, threatening to engulf her. Dead fields seemed to stretch on forever. Even the graffiti on the faded roadside billboards had grown sparse. Only true believers dared to tread this far into a diffusion zone.

A blistering red glow crept through the haze ahead. Harper's step faltered as the growing impulse to crawl away to a different reality gnawed at her stomach. Madison grabbed her hand, helping her put one foot in front of the other. As she moved deeper into the maroon fog, the gleam took shape. On the side of the road, there was a rundown motel aglow with neon lights.

A sickly man sat behind the front desk, preoccupied by the machine in front of him. It was a kitbashed piece of work: a small cathode-ray tube television with a DIY tape player hooked on top. Clear cables pulsing with iridescent fluid ran the length of the CRT's body. One stretched away from the machine into an implant in the clerk's neck. On the small display, Harper could see degraded images from the old world – a woman undressing in a pristine apartment decades before her time. She felt the impulse again, fidgeting slightly as she imagined being embodied in a tape experience herself. She hadn't gotten a chance in over a day, and neither had Madison. He pounded his fist on the service bell. The phosphorescent display powered off and the tube ripped away from the clerk's neck with a wet pop. He doubled over in his chair, gasping for air.

"Can I help you?" the clerk wheezed.

"We want a room for the night," said Madison.

"Trying to cross the veil?" he said with a chuckle, which quickly turned into a cough.

"Something like that," said Harper. "I can pay with ichor." She pulled a vial of the iridescent fluid from the pocket of her thick coat and placed it on the counter. The clerk pocketed it with desperation in his eyes, and held out the key to room seventeen.

Madison snatched the key and stepped outside. Harper followed him along the side of the crumbling motel, observing the vines consuming the building as they neared their room. Inside, there was an unmade bed, a broken nightstand, and a cracked mirror affixed to a disintegrating wall. She caught an unwilling glimpse of her reflection in the distorted glass. As usual, she thought she barely looked human. A cracked radio in the corner hissed a stream of degraded rock music and choppy news broadcasts mixed with a harsh drone track laid underneath – a genre that had come to be called frag. Madison switched the radio off, then slung his backpack off his shoulder. From it, he removed a machine similar to the clerk's and placed it on the bed. The screen flickered on and a cheery synthesizer jingle emanated from its soldered-on speakers. Harper closed the door and sighed in relief. Finally, the impulse could be satisfied.

She let her jacket fall to the floor, followed by her cargo pants. She hesitated as she lifted her top, stopping before exposing the first modification in her torso. The heat of Madison's body radiated against her back as he approached, undressed, with a tube from the machine on the bed pumping radiant fluid into his neck. He looked at her with cloudy eyes, his mind already drifting away from reality. She spared a glance toward the broken mirror, watching as he softly grabbed the hem of her shirt and pulled it over her head.

"You're beautiful," he said. Harper didn't believe him.

His hands ran down her bare abdomen, fingertips circling the mods jutting from her chest and stomach. Some were necessary for her to survive, regulating bodily functions and supplying missing hormones. Many increased the efficacy of the machine erupting from her abdomen – a black box with an opening for the narrow cassettes of the tape experiences, and two tubes of ichor which curved into the flesh of her stomach. Harper could not remember a time before her first modifications. They had always kept her alive in spite of the way she was born.

Harper's breath hitched as Madison inserted a tape into her abdominal modification. She adjusted to the weight of it inside her. Madison guided her to lay down on the ragged motel sheets. She felt a tight pull, followed by a sudden release deep within her body as the tape began to play. Warmth rushed through her veins. The machine whirred and rumbled softly against her flesh. Madison embraced her, and time melted away as the two lay skin to skin, each lost in unremembered windows of the past.

EXT. SUBURB STREET—DAY

Everything in the world is alive. The texture of surfaces dance with grain and the sky bursts with chromatic aberrations. There is a quaint, white house before me with a lawn and a tire swing. This is a world defined by abundance rather than absence.

I look down at my body. My flesh is unmodified. I have no implants here. I am entirely organic. Natural. Correct.

MARY

Harper? We've been waiting for you!

MARY idles at the front door with a wide smile. I feel compelled to approach, as I always do.

INT. HOUSE—DAY
I have been in this house many times. There's something comforting about the unchanging geometry of its off-white walls and beige carpet. There is a safety I have never experienced in my twenty-seven years of life. It is alien to the violence and decay of the settlement I grew up in.

I follow Mary past the basement door and up the carpeted stairs.

INT. NURSERY—DAY
There is a crib with a newborn child inside. He is perfect.

MARY
Do you want to hold him?

I nod and move closer to the crib. I catch a glimpse of myself in the mirror on the wall. I look happy.

Before I can reach in, the world before me splinters apart into a gaping void. Words flash before my eyes.

YOU ARE AWAITED.
YOU ARE AWAITED.
YOU ARE AWAITED.

I'm coming. You know I'm coming.
Let me go back. Please.

INT. NURSERY—DAY
Carefully, I lift the child into my arms. I feel that all is right with the world.

Harper watched the sunrise through the window slats, cradled in Madison's arms. She was still pressed against him in the bed, though the fluid from both of their machines had run out hours before. She trailed her fingers along his bare forearm, tracing his veins, caressing his sticky skin beneath her fingertips.

"What are you thinking about?" he mumbled groggily.

"When was the last time you saw a kid? In the real world, I mean."

"Five or six weeks ago in Ampess, I think," Madison replied.

"I keep wondering what it'd be like to raise one," she said. "With you."

"It's wrong to bring a kid into this world," he said.

Harper rolled out from beneath his arms and sat upright. "Probably a good thing I can't

have 'em. They'd just turn out like me anyways."

Madison's hand brushed against her back. "Things will be different on the other side. We'll have everything we're missing," he said. "There'll be air and trees and . . . we can go back to living the way people are meant to."

"I know we will. We have to." Harper blinked back tears, refusing to face him. "I'm so tired of being an abomination."

"Hey, look at me," he said softly. Harper's gaze lifted to meet his. "You're the only thing worth a damn on this futureless rock."

Her eyes darted away, focusing on a tear in the wallpaper. She couldn't face the sincerity in his eyes. It was the same sincerity that convinced her to leave the Telexan slums years earlier; sincerity she thought she didn't deserve until she was reborn on the other side of the veil.

When they took their first steps beyond the motel that morning, Harper saw a body strung up on the power lines. She hadn't noticed him before in the dark. Little remained besides bone and metal. She felt jealous; his soul was part of the grid, free from the implants stuck in his withered flesh. Madison didn't seem to notice the man, and as they walked, he disappeared in the distance behind them. The day passed quickly and the night fell without warning as they neared an array of transmission towers blinking with red lights, like dozens of eyes watching them grow closer to their final destination. Harper returned the gaze of her silent voyeurs. As she did, a high pitched whine pierced through her mind. She registered a pop somewhere inside and hoped that it wouldn't affect anything important – but it wouldn't have mattered if it did. The sensitivity of her implant was a good sign. It meant they were getting close. Through her blurred vision, she saw the road in front of her dissolve into the ground as if being reclaimed by the dirt. She barely registered Madison grabbing her arm and jerking her toward him. Bit by bit, the whine faded and her vision came back into focus. The road ahead had crumbled away into a sheer dropoff.

"Shit, Harp!" Madison said. "How the hell did you not see that cliff? It was . . . "

He fell silent as he gazed into the abyss with Harper. In the muted red light of the distant towers, they could see a slanted gravel path lined with electrical poles leading into the gorge. At the bottom, there was a cathedral built of stone brick and stained glass. The building was so perfectly situated within the rocky hollow that it was impossible to tell if it had been placed there by divine intervention or unearthed by human curiosity long ago. Based on the uneven ground it sat upon, the Earth was keen to swallow it either way.

"Ready to leave this godforsaken place?" Harper asked, breathless.

Madison nodded. He held her hand as they trudged down the steep path. A graveyard of rusted televisions, broken tape recorders, melted generators, and jagged machinery half-buried in the ground lined the walkway to the holy structure. As they grew nearer, the massive wooden doors creaked open. Beyond the threshold, there was only darkness. Harper was the first to step into the narthex. Cables snaked through every inch of the stone hall, wrapping around corners and dangling from the ceiling. The murals on the walls were chipped and fading. This was a place of both the old world and the new; a centuries-old monument once meant for God, now reverent only to machines.

Harper drifted toward the entrance to the nave. She held her breath as she passed through into the large chamber with Madison in lock-step. The former place of worship was in disarray, with nests of wires trailing down the walls and rumbling pipes running along the ceiling. Murals made of coiled metal and circuitry in the shape of human bodies lined the aisles. One displayed a man perpetually screaming with his chest flayed open, exposing organs made of silver machinery. Another showed an infant suspended by steel cables. Harper slowed to a halt as they neared the sanctuary. The altar was blanketed by dark shadows, but she could make out a silhouette behind it.

"Do you see that statue?" Harper whispered.

The statue moved. Behind the altar, a wall of CRT screens lit up with blue-grey static. The silhouette grew more defined. It wore silver robes and a white mask with gold etchings. The gloves running up into its sleeves and the hood over its head left no skin exposed.

"We have been waiting for you, Harper," the figure said. "My designation is Matron. I am the priestess of this sanctuary."

"We're here to cross the phosphorescent veil," said Madison. "Can you help us?"

"Only one of you will cross the veil," said Matron.

A cable dropped from the ceiling and curled toward Madison with a mind of its own. It wrapped around his neck and coupled with his implant, then glowed softly, transporting ichor into his veins. Harper watched powerlessly as Madison dropped to the ground. One of the screens behind Matron flickered to a perspective of a verdant forest in the old world. She stepped out from behind the altar. "We have recalled all carriers to fulfill their purpose."

Harper was frozen in place. "Carriers?" she whispered.

"Those who have given their flesh to us. You are modified to our specifications," the priestess said, strolling toward Harper. "Do you know what is on the other side of the phosphorescent veil?"

"Some say it's a way back to the old world," she said, trembling. "A world with a future."

"There is no future to be built from the old world, and there is no returning to it—only simulacrums," said Matron. "The other side is where tape experiences originate. Where ichor comes from, brought to our side through transductive rifts."

"If it's not the old world then what's on the other side?" Harper asked.

"Radiant creatures," said Matron. "Creatures that hear and see and laugh and cry just like we do. They long for a new home." Harper backed away from the priestess, eyes brimming with tears, locked onto her unblinkingly. Her foot snagged on a cable running through the walkway and she tripped, falling onto her back. Matron stepped toward Harper, towering over her on the ground. "Do you want children?"

"Madison says it's wrong. That it would be cruel because this world is ruined."

"He doesn't appreciate the ability he has," Matron hissed. "But you would."

"I gave up that ability so I could live," Harper said through gritted teeth.

"You do not have to choose anymore," the priestess purred. "You can finally be what you have always wanted. You can do what you were meant to do. Don't you want children, Harper?"

"More than anything."

"You've given so much of yourself in exchange for life. How much more are you willing to give?"

Harper stared at the dark eyeholes of the white mask above her, searching for a trace of humanity in the priestess. Her eyes darted around the nave, across the murals on the wall and the glowing cables running along the floor. There was a gnawing feeling in her stomach, and an impulse tugging at every piece of machinery in her body.

"All of it."

Harper rose to her feet. From the ceiling, a mess of metal, tubes, and cables spiraled toward the ground in a conical shape, terminating in a large black plug just below her eye level. Matron tapped her on the shoulder. Harper turned.

"You are creating the future," said the priestess. She reached behind Harper's head and gripped the plug, then jammed it into the port in the back of her neck. Deep inside, she felt a pull, then a sudden release.

INT. HOUSE—NIGHT

The house is empty. Mary is gone, but the basement door lays open. This has never happened before. It fills me with dread.

A distorted choir sings deep below my feet, and I know that there is only one path forward. I step into the dark.

INT. BASEMENT—NIGHT
The staircase stretches on for longer than I thought possible, descending deeper and deeper below the Earth.

Finally, the stairs open out into an unfinished cellar. The stone walls are cracked, and the fluorescent lights hum softly overhead. There is a dirty mattress in the center of the room. The child lies on it.

I lift him into my arms. This is everything I have ever wanted.

The foundation shakes. The walls crumble around us.

INT. BASEMENT—THE OTHER SIDE OF THE VEIL
We remain enclosed by a cage of writhing cables. They contort around us into the shape of four walls and a ceiling. I do not feel afraid. I belong here.

A black rectangular doorway blinks into existence. The man from the powerline shambles through. His withered skin barely clings to his skeletal frame. He stares at me with synthetic eyes. Slowly, like a marionette controlled by strings, he gestures to the doorway. Words flash in my field of vision.

STEP INTO YOUR FUTURE.
STEP INTO YOUR FUTURE.
STEP INTO YOUR FUTURE.

The choir sings on the other side of the doorway. I step forward with the child still in my arms. The man cocks his head.

LEAVE IT.
LEAVE IT.
LEAVE IT.

ME
The priestess said I would have a child. I've given everything for this.

The man places his cold, stiff hand on my shoulder.

YOU WILL HAVE WHAT YOU ARE MISSING.
YOU WILL HAVE WHAT YOU ARE MISSING.
YOU WILL HAVE WHAT YOU ARE MISSING.

I put the child down. Its skin glows and peels away, dissolving into the mattress. When it is gone, I step through the doorway.

INT. CATHEDRAL—NIGHT
There is a restless jitter over the world. The cathedral is hazy with grain. I see myself from the outside, jacked into the machine descending from the ceiling through the main port on my neck and several tubes plugged into my other implants.

Madison is on the ground, plugged into an experience of his own. I take comfort in the fact that his mind is suspended in a peaceful vision of the past. One with trees. He would have liked that.

I approach myself. My skin is glowing as the tubes pump ichor into my bloodstream. It is dissolving my tissue, burning through me from the inside out. The metal beneath my skin becomes visible as my flesh melts. The ichor carries the broken down material away as fuel for my implants, which remain in place.

I feel none of this. The process goes on for hours.

INT. CHAPTER HOUSE—NIGHT
Metal tendrils lay my body against the wall next to a dozen corpses. The machinery in my stomach is exposed through my dissolved anatomy: a number of organ modifications and the inner workings of the device for tape experiences. The grotesque machines whir and rumble against what remains of my flesh, filling the room with sickening squelches. Matron stands with two others dressed like her. They stare at my body twitching against the wall, waiting for something.

My body falls still. Something crawls from my mangled stomach. It is a mess of tissue and bone, red viscera bound together with wires and transistors. The abomination's eyes are black and beady, with a warped mouth that resembles a beak more than human lips. An inhuman sound comes from the orifice; a gasping scream from lungs without air. It is the sound of a creature new to this world.

A black doorway appears in front of me. I turn my head. The man from the powerline watches.

YOU WILL BE REMADE AS ONE OF US.
YOU WILL BE REMADE AS ONE OF US.
YOU WILL BE REMADE AS ONE OF US.

I know this world is no longer mine. This is how things must be.

I step through the doorway.

EXT. THE OTHER SIDE OF THE VEIL
The sky is dark. There is a flat plain before me made not of Earth but of circuits and synthetic tendrils. They writhe through the ground, carrying pulses of light, like blood from arteries, to a monolith in the distance. The spire of organic matter erupts from the metallic surface of this place. The tendrils carry the pulses up its length, consuming it, powering capacitors embedded in the pink tissue.

Eyes open in the firmament above. There are a thousand pupils in the dark watching me without blinking. This place teems with radiant creatures. I feel comforted by their presence.

The monolith sings. Its voice is a chorus of thousands, all rejoicing because I have become like them. I have given everything for it.

I march toward the monolith, and I feel that all is right with the world.

Pareidolia

ASHE THURMAN

PHILOCTETES MISSION 5-PILOT VIDEO LOG
Audio Transcription by [REDACTED]
06.03.2030
Speaker: Dr. Casey Holden

Alright. let it be known that I much prefer to do these logs in text versus video but whatever. That was the directive. It is what it is.

We're at the end of the first day of space day in NRHO around the moon. Orbiting the moon not gonna lie it is pretty ******* cool. I will be swearing in these; deal with it.

So this is extremely cool obviously. I've done the ISS. I've done some satellite repair missions, but this . . . God, this is just incredible.

You know, I had this interview right before we launched where they asked, you know, why am I doing this? Why are you doing this solo mission? And I gave a nice little, you know, pretty PR answer about *oh! science* and *isn't just thinking it's doing* and *reach for the stars*, but it's money. It's all about money. And not even my money like their money. We wanna start doing mythium lining . . . lithium mining on the moon and to make that profitable you have to figure out how to do it as efficiently as possible. So if you can design a mining rig that you run by one or two people you're gonna cut your cost immensely.

The thing is, though, we know what solitude does to the human brain. Do we need to continue to test it by throwing ships into space? I'm trying to sort of grasp that part, still.

Yet I applied for the program here I am, so what's that say about me?

06.09.2030
Speaker: Dr. Casey Holden, Capsule Voice Alert

HOLDEN
I'm supposed to be doing these logs everyday and I'm not. This is why they should be written.

CVA
Alert: dorsal fuselage integrity

HOLDEN
And that needs to be more specific or overridable. It's an external heat plate. I'm going to walk to fix it tomorrow. Until then—

CVA
Alert: dorsal fuselage integrity

HOLDEN
Oh, my God, I know.

06.11.2030
Speaker: Dr. Casey Holden

I had the weirdest dream last night—sleep cycle. I'm in a car with my dad, but he's not actually in the car with me, he's somewhere else. Dream logic. And and we're—we're arguing about something and then the car explodes and then there's cheese everywhere. And I tend to dream in abstraction so this is surprisingly concrete for my typical dreams. I also haven't had a driving dream since the Air Force, so that was, you know, a fun little trip now memory lane.

But it's also, I think, the first time I've dreamed about my dad since he died. He resented the **** out of me for coming into the military as a commissioned officer while he had to work up the ranks. But that's not my fault. I didn't do that. I don't even necessarily agree with that organizational structure. Which, like, is the military gonna come for me, now? What are they gonna do: not send me to space? Whatever. This is why I shouldn't do video logs. I'm a yapper.

So, yeah, like I purposely try not to think about him so that's why I don't normally dream about him, but up here there's nothing else to think about so I'm thinking about him and then bam I dream about him. So it's a whole thing, I guess.

Oh, and while I am thinking about it the customizable daylight program we have on this mission is the best one I've had. My circadian rhythm's always been off from everyone else, so I like that I get to set it to what I want. Keep that going forward.

06.13.2030
Speaker: Dr. Casey Holden

If my calendar date is correct it's my birthday. Happy birthday to me. Forty-five, no spouse, no kids, but then that's what makes this mission so much better. Give me an escape from all those people asking me when I was gonna settle down. Even my fellow astronauts.

Sally Ride had to hide her wife for 30 years. I can't even put a gender-neutral pronoun down on my application without worrying that they're gonna kick me out of NASA. Like, for being a bunch of scientists we're real **** with that.

Like, stay on Earth and be openly out, or go to space. In that scenario who wouldn't pick go to space? Seems like a super easy decision to make.

06.17.2030
Speaker: Dr. Casey Holden

OK I was listening back to one of my previous video logs and I think I lied to you a little bit. Seeing the moon out of the porthole all the time, I actually kind of miss a natural night time. It always have this very, like, liminal quality to me. Like it's extra time to exist in the world that you aren't being looked at and judged and all that ****. Anyway.

I am experiencing a little more auditory pareidolia than I anticipated. It's sort of kicked up the past two days. There's so much stuff here that creates white noise I don't know which specific thing is triggering it. Gonna do a little poking around to see if I can pinpoint. Could be some interesting data.

06.23.2030
Speaker: Dr. Casey Holden

OK so I cannot figure out what is causing the specific noise I'm hearing. I did a bunch of like power ups and power downs on some equipment around the ship to try to, like, troubleshoot what was making the sound and I—I don't know. I don't know what it is. But this... this is the reason why this one person mission idea is dead in the water.

I recognize that we're a couple iterations into this project and so the ship is technically designed to run with one crew member. But what if this had been the life support system I was trying to fix? Sometimes you just need more than one set of hands to do anything, this is ridiculous.

I think I sound angrier than I actually, and I'm just taking it out on the video. But my point stands.

06.25.2030
Speaker: Dr. Casey Holden, Capsule Voice Alert

HOLDEN
The music package that we created for this project is not good enough. plenty of music, but we need to add podcasts or audio plays or something. Feel like I'm forgetting what words sound like, and it's making the pareidolia, worse.

CVA
Alert: radial drop

HOLDEN
Thank you, Computer.

Now I have to go figure out what's wrong with my orbit, if anything.

This is still a terrible alert system.

07.02.2030
Speaker: Dr. Casey Holden

If they actually want this to be a long term project they're gonna need to figure out something better than the ******* vacuum clippers. I went full buzz cut just so I wouldn't have to deal with them, but I'm at that point where when you touch it, it's weird, you know what I mean. So I can only imagine if you had long hair.

'Cause I've always been just cut it all off instead of dealing with it kind of person. Which really ****** my mom off back when I was a kid because "oh your curls!" But I just . . . I don't I don't give a **** anymore. Just chop chop chop.

That kind of thing's actually probably what drove me to space to begin with, you know. You see *Pale Blue Do*t for the first time and all you can think is "Oh well OK none of this earth **** matters." Just this-just a sack of blood and organs and electrical signals moving through the world. Everything else is just **** we made-up to create order out of chaos.

You know, that's how I should have answered that one interview question.

"To get away from it all. Not to deal with it for a little while."

07.12.2030
Speaker: Dr. Casey Holden

OK, cool so I'm beginning to think that these are actual auditory hallucinations and not just pareidolia. Obviously, I can't do the psychiatric diagnostic stuff, but I did some troubleshooting with my noise canceling headphones. I can hear the voice through the headphones.

So what I am specifically hearing is this kind of like . . . a flange effect voice. Maybe chorus? Kind of mid range androgynous. Very neutral voice. Very monotone. But the thing is like the sound I'm actually hearing doesn't physically sound like words, but I also somehow understand them. Like my mind is assigning meaning to the sounds I'm hearing. And the words themselves are-are not . . . they're random. OK well . . . not really random . . . like . . . they're space words. But it's kind of like a toddler walks into a room, and it's just pointing at things and saying what they are. That's what it feels like.

I'm not experiencing any paranoia. I recognize that these are hallucinations. No visual hallucinations. No other physiological symptoms. I'm keeping a very detailed medical log Otherwise, though, like, I feel fine, that's the thing. So I'm gonna try a few different things like techniques to sort of like manage what I'm experiencing and, uh, yeah. This is actually like a pretty interesting phenomenon to observe from a scientific perspective

07.13.2030
Speaker: Dr. Casey Holden

So last night I had another one of those really weird dreams. On Earth, I have pretty vivid dreams, that I mostly remember. In space, not as much. That's why that dream about my dad stood out. The one I had last night, though, holy ****.

So remember that part of contact where Jodie Foster meets the alien but the alien is like taking the form of her dad. That was the dream I had. I was Jodie Foster and the dad-alien was my dad. Only the alien told me that they took the form of my dad specifically because he's the one who would piss me off the most. And I asked the alien, you know, why are you trying to make me mad. Like what's the point of that. And the alien says oh I just thought it'd be funny. But like I have this sensation that the alien was trying to sort of understand what humans were like and like how to push my buttons, I guess. Like testing limits. Then I woke up mad.

So I went back and looked at the heart rate data from my suit, and, yeah, there was definitely a whole bunch of spikes right around when I feel like this dream might have taken place. But it's also kind of odd that I have any sensation of when the dream took place at all. Because I didn't wake up from the dream if that makes sense. Like I had the dream but then I kept sleeping and then I woke up. Or at least that's how I perceived it, right.

I think for the next missions we should definitely find a way to incorporate some kind of brain wave monitoring. Because I feel like that's going to give us some very interesting data around things like R.E.M. sleep or just any kind of brain wave activity. 'Cause I feel like—I feel like there's something happening here that I don't have the proper equipment to monitor it. So definitely a consideration for additional missions going forward, I think.

07.25.2030
Speaker: Dr. Casey Holden

OK so the voice is starting to put together more complex phrases and sort of word pairs. And I'm disinclined to call them complete thoughts necessarily. I'm definitely seeing some like predicate-subject combos, but they're not, you know, in grammatical agreement necessarily. But that's actually the weirdest part to me right now. Because I'm still not hearing actual words. I'm still hearing non-word sounds and understanding them. So if my brain is ascribing meaning to the sounds, why am I not inherently automatically making them grammatically correct. Like, does that question make sense?

You know, what's—what's the opposite of the Chinese room? 'Cause I feel like that's what's happening here. I'm having a really hard time describing what I'm experiencing . There just . . . there's no-there's no words for it already in existence. You know, I can't be experiencing a completely new phenomenon. Someone else has to have experiences this before. But did they also lack the language to describe what was happening to them? Is this Moses and the burning bush?

I don't know. It's it's freaking me out I'm not gonna lie. I'm gonna be extremely candid in that regard. At the same time, consider the psychiatric applications. You know, what if this is some kind of a solar radiation damage that we just never experienced before? Like I have some weird genetic quirk where solar radiation activates a part of my brain that we . . . associate with something like . . . schizophrenia . . . or cluster B personality disorder. What if there is some kind of connection we can make to improve treatments for those because of this,

Like, this is not what I set out to do coming up here, but, God, if we can get something like that from this, how absolutely incredible would that be. So, like I said I'm gonna keep doing my very detailed medical logs. I'm gonna try to make these video logs more detailed, as well, because I really want to make sure we have as much record of this phenomenon as possible.

07.30.2030
Speaker: Dr. Casey Holden, Capsule Voice Alert

CVA
Alert: water recycling system integrity

HOLDEN
Oh, my God, shut up, I know.

So, some things I've tried so far to sort of deal with these hallucinations are kind of around, I guess you could say, tricking my auditory system. I chose to bring up a lot of instrumental music, so I'm trying to focus more on the actual vocal music instead to see if I can't figure out what pathways these hallucinations might be using. I'm also attempting to talk to myself more. I'm sort of narrating my day like "oh take this pipette and put it here" or "what an interesting thing I'm seeing on this agar plate" or "oh that's interesting, you know, cell cluster." My thinking being that maybe my brain is so starved for structured speech it's trying to create its own perhaps. Something beyond basic pattern recognition.

And this is such a duct tape and cardboard approach the whole situation, but if I don't have a psychiatrist or a psychologist or a neurologist to talk to, I don't know what I'm meant to do about it. This is all well beyond my area of expertise.

And so, again, I think that speaks to the problems inherent to a solo mission. In any kind of long term project you have no idea what kind of obstacles you're going to face. So if you don't have a team that can sort of cover all those bases, how do you expect to see long term effectiveness in the middle of ******* space.

Like, I'm looking at the moon out of my porthole hearing voices in my head. That is an absolutely ridiculous situation for anyone to be in. So at least if I—you know, blow my brains out up here you'll have a journal to look back on and go "oh OK This is why we shouldn't do this."

08.04.2030
Speaker: Dr. Casey Holden

So the voice is talking to me, now. Before it was just—it was just words. It was...it was words that didn't really have a lot of connected meaning, and now it is forming sentences and talking directly to me. It's very complimentary. The voice is still very monotone, still very neutral, still very androgynous, but it's saying nice things. "That suit looks lovely on you." Which it very much doesn't, so it's not even telling the truth.

And I think if it was just that. I could handle it 'cause it's clearly my brain just trying to create order out of chaos. It's just trying to escalate the sensation to the next logical conclusion that I understand in terms of how language works. But the voice also seems to have a directionality to it. You know, before I feel like I was just sort of hearing it around me all the time. Now, it's more like I'll be standing in one place and I will hear the voice from this specific part of the ship to my right. Then I move away from it, and it follows me, and now it's on my left. But I can I can trace the path of it moving. It doesn't talk while it moves, but I can sense it moving from this place to this place as far as like triangulating where the sound is coming from. And it sounds like it's on the outside of the ship. Like-like there's a thing hanging on the outside of the ship, and then just crawling across the outer hull when I move through the ship. Like it's following me.

Is—is that paranoia? Like is that what that symptom sounds like and feels like and looks like? 'Cause I don't feel like it's threatening me. I don't feel like it wishes me harm.

But, now, I . . . I don't know—I don't know how to handle this.

08.07.2030
Speaker: Dr. Casey Holden

The voices started asking me questions. It wants to know who am I, what species am I from, why am I in space, why am I at the moon, specifically. "Oh what's that you're doing there at the at the workbench with the microscope." And it knows what a microscope is it—it used the word microscope. I mean, it didn't actually use the word microscope it said whatever the ******* sound it makes that I understood to mean microscope.

This—this was—this was kind of cool at first. This was kind of an interesting psychiatric issue I was experiencing because it wasn't particularly distressing. I can recognize that oh hey I'm experiencing a slew of symptoms ,but I know that's not reality, so I'm OK.

That assurance is slipping away a little bit. Because I don't know what my brain is doing. It is rearranging reality around me, and I don't know if I can trust it. I've never been particularly connected to my body, but this is . . . I don't even recognize anything about myself anymore.

How do I know that I can do the job I'm up here to do and keep myself safe if this is what my brain is doing? The stakes here are too damn high.

08.11.2030
Speaker: Dr. Casey Holden

**** it I've started answering its questions. They're good questions. They show intelligence and curiosity and the ability to sort of put context clues together and create follow up conversation. Anyway, I'm actually finding what's most difficult is answering questions in a way that kind of satisfies it. Because I'm coming in with all this cultural baggage that it doesn't have.

Like I got a little hung up when I was trying to describe sexual dimorphism until I realized it doesn't know what a man versus a woman is. I could just hit it with, you know, oocyte producing organ, and they understand that.

<<12 second of silence>>

It's asking me right now who I'm talking to. So now I'm gonna have to explain that I'm talking into a video camera to communicate with more people back on Earth and just hope that it it understood that . . .

OK cool great cool you understand that. You understand that I'm making a—the talking to Earth part you don't understand . . .

It's like radio communication . . . I've explained that one . . . So this is like that but film. I haven't explained—

It doesn't understand film . . . okay . . .

CABIN FOOTAGE-CAMERA 3
Audio Transcription by [REDACTED]
08.26.2030
Speakers: Dr. Casey Holden, Capsule Voice Alert, Unknown

HOLDEN
I told you, I need the helmet. Hold on.

CVA
Airlock interior door activated.

HOLDEN
Wow you are . . . huh . . .
No I'm not latched I can't I can't really come further out.

UNKNOWN
[unintelligible]

HOLDEN
I mean I can maybe get a little bit closer let me just—

UNKNOWN
[unintelligible]

CVA
Airlock exterior door activated.

UNKNOWN
[unintelligible]

<<STATIC AUDIO INTERFERENCE>>

CVA
Alert: airlock open

Alert: airlock open

Alert: airlock open

we'll grow fast like weeds, baby

ZIGGY SCHUTZ

Remember
when your mother called me a weed?

It was right after she caught us kissing on your bed, babe. She insisted it wasn't my tits that made her so angry (and they make me angry too, sometimes, although not for the same reasons), but my lack of plans for the future that had her banning me from darkening your doorstep.

And, yeah. Still haven't caught any of those. Plans for the future, I mean.

But I have things growing in me
nonetheless, through my trauma like through
cracks in concrete. Dandelion crowns peek out
from underneath my nails.
I've started to cry things with thorns.

Does it still count as me getting soft, darling, when my expressions of emotion often lead to awkwardly placed bandaids? Like that summer we both tried to learn how to skateboard, colourful plasters over our cheeks and elbows, a bouquet of little mistakes and stories to tell.

I hope I'm softer.
I'm tired of callouses and bulbs that never bloom.
You make me want to open up.
You make everything smell like spring, so
how else am I supposed to respond but
with open petals?

I'll come to pick you up for the last time, tonight. My tongue is heavy with that moss you love, the kind you used as a pillow, that time when you were thirteen and ran away from home for the first time.

(remember in science class, back in fifth grade, when they told us plants have their own ideas of gender? That must be what the first rain feels like, for little seedlings. Exactly like that. Like the moment they realize there's a whole world out there, even when they're all buried in the earth)

We'll do it right, this time. No getting dragged back. No mothers screaming. Just us, blown to the wind, letting it take us far, far away.

Somewhere with sun.
Together. After all,
us weeds can grow
wherever we land.

She Calls Me Love

Lyd Low

"Good morning, love." She murmurs into my hair. Our limbs are tangled together like the roots of an old tree that has always been. We each have our own pillows, but in the morning we always manage to find ourselves crammed onto the same one. It is an island of warmth, and softness. Hair tickles nostrils. Breath tickles skin. There is no world beyond these shores. Or at least that was what I try to believe as I hesitate on the edge of waking.

"Pie," is all I can muster, not quite ready for the morning.

"Coffee first, love?"

"Please."

She pulls herself up, if only so she can see me in the entirety of my dismantled glory. I allow it. It's a miracle she still finds me charming. A miracle I am grateful for.

I am eventually bribed out of our nest of blankets by the promise of her happy hums as she putters about. Our favorite mug is filled, chasing the cold from my hands. She seals the warmth into me with a languorous kiss. Her lips are sticky, and sweet. She always licks the spoon after stirring honey into our coffee.

It is useful (and dangerous) to live above our favorite cafe. Acquiring pie only requires the barest pretense of clothing. Today it's the type of oversized shirt that used to be black but had been washed and worn into a tired gray. It's long enough that we don't bother with pants. We never stay long, and always tip well.

The stares are hard to ignore. I press myself closer against her as the neon-haired barista packs up our order. The scent of her hair dissolves my knots of anxiety. No one else matters outside of us.

Pie was secured. We could return to the apartment. Our apartment. I know we used to have our own places. I must have been elated when she first gave me a spare key, but our lives had slid so seamlessly together that I hardly remember those days. I do wonder how many firsts I've forgotten, whittled from monumental moments into endless grains of sand on the beach of our bliss.

"You are my everything." I say when it is just us again. It is an unshakable truth, but I still enjoy the sensation of the words. She smiles, and feeds me a forkful of pie.

"And you are mine, love." She says back, before leaning in to lick a smudge of rhubarb from the corner of my mouth. I dissolve into giggles, and she chases my peals of laughter with kisses.

We make love on the kitchen counter until the last of the morning chill melts into cloying afternoon heat. It's too humid to snuggle, but we can't bear to be properly apart. We settle on splaying out on the carpet on our backs, our shoulders grazing each other. I can feel the heat coming off her skin. Her fingers dance along my arm. I can almost pretend everything is fine, but my pulse races away from hers. A tear runs from the corner of my eye into hers.

"It's going to get worse, you know."

"I know, love. It's okay."

It wasn't. But I was too much of a coward to push her away.

It was the ribs we noticed first. One day one of her ribs was just gone. My fingers had chanced upon the soft valley where it used to be. There was no bruise, no blood. I inspected my own chest as she watched, standing behind me, arms circled around my waist. There it was, in my own chest. I screamed, and clawed at it. She had calmed me down enough for us to get to the ER. The nurses were confused, but didn't seem to share our alarm. I kept the X-rays. Her nine ribs glowing against my eleven.

Next were the nails. She held up shaky hands to reveal my nervously chewed nails, so out of place against her elegant fingers. I looked down to find her neatly manicured pinks sitting at odds with my calloused knuckles.

The teeth were the hardest to get used to.

Any answers we cobbled together from online wanderings stopped at the psychological, and shed little light on our physical transmutations. Whenever we offered any details of ourselves, we were met with cold skepticism, or a hungry curiosity that reeked of danger. We gave up on searching, or asking. There was no real reason to. The changes were strange, but it didn't cause us pain. For a moment, I wondered if it was our very closeness that was the cause, but even considering separation felt like a kind of death. This was better.

We soon lost track of whose parts were whose. Did I always have these freckles? Did she always have that mole? I watched as she treated her new parts with a tenderness I could never have extended to myself. I did my best to show the new parts I now housed with all the affection and reverence I did when they were still hers.

Eventually our changes became too hard to explain to other people, and they always asked while their concerned gazes scoured our bodies. They were so fixated on where she ended, and I began. It was unbearable. We stopped showing up, or answering messages. No one else could possibly understand what we were going through. It didn't matter. We had each other. Eventually we stopped leaving our apartment altogether. A few clicks and everything could be delivered. Even pie. We didn't have to leave.

Coffee, pie, sex, and cuddles. Repeat into oblivion.

The line between us became so inconsequential that when the tally of our parts began to dwindle, it seemed as natural as the shifting of seasons. One morning there was simply one lung in each chest. One eye in each head. Eventually the sum of our ribs knitted themselves together to cradle our single heart. Anything that was extraneous simply ceased to be. We learned to walk again. It was a wonder that we ever needed four legs. Everyday actions that had seemed so banal before became a new way for us to grow, dance, and feel. Her skin was my skin. My blood was hers. I traced my levees with her fingertips. She swirled her eddies with my tongue.

The names were the last to go. A wine glass slips from our grasp. It crashes down to a floor that feels miles away. Blood roars in our ears.

"My name. What was it?" The brutal realization barrels me over. I couldn't take in enough air. How could I forget my own name? Had I forgotten hers? How much had I lost?

She Calls Me Love

Her hand, my hand, runs soothingly through our hair. We know what a panic attack looks like from both sides of the glass. Our body rocks slowly, cradled in our arms.

"Love. That is our name." Each word is articulated slowly, carving out a fresh truth we had somehow always known. The panic ebbs away. That panicked rabbit's pace belongs to a distant heart. The singular warmth that pulsed within our chest knows no such fear. We are love. All is well. There is no world beyond these shores.

We weep without sadness. We smile as we wipe away our tears. We fall back onto the couch, picking up the remote, flipping through the carousel of choices. We settle on our favorite. We laugh at the familiar jokes. We nestle into our arms. We drift into dreams in tandem.

"Good night, love." We murmur into our hair. Our limbs tangle together. The roots of a tree that has always been.

I Sing the Body Celestial

MAXIM VOLK

There are no mirrors in my house because seeing a glimpse of my reflection is torment. I do not allow myself to be photographed. There should be no evidence that I exist for others to look upon. I am not meant to be here. I am not meant to be me.

I try in vain to imagine a body in which I feel comfortable. I picture myself more masculine, with rugged features and a jawline that could cut steel, and I nearly vomit. I visualize a more feminine body, with soft lips and long flowing hair, and I despise that as well. Piece by piece, like a doll with interchangeable parts, I pull the bits of me away and replace them with other segments of other bodies. Those, too, repel me. There is no version of myself that I would be partial to; no body in which I can abide.

I have always felt like a stranger in my own existence. As a child, I would scream at my father that I wanted to change who I was, to be someone else. I would ask my mother when I would receive a new body, and she would laugh at the implication. At night, I would stare up at the stars, wondering if there was anyone like me observing these same celestial bodies. Surely, I cannot be the only one. Surely, I am not alone.

Today, like every day, I force myself to dress and walk to work. Every time I catch myself in a store window or see my face in a puddle below my feet, I grimace at the sight of myself. My pale, fleshy face stares back at me, and I do not recognize it. At the office, my colleagues greet me by name, and I forget for a moment that it is mine. It should not be mine. My name is not that short two-syllable sound with which these people refer to me. My name is not something that could be uttered by any living being. It is something beyond human language.

On an ordinary day, as much as any day can be ordinary, my office is drab and empty, more so with me in it. Today, however, it is occupied by someone the likes of whom I have never seen before. She is ethereal, standing taller than me, with hair the color of night and skin like porcelain. Her body is lithe and long, and she slithers across the couch on which she sits, welcoming me with a nod. Her red lips speak my name, and though the words do not describe me, the sound of it feels at home.

"I have a proposition for you," she whispers, her voice gravelly. "There is some business I would like you to attend to. Something that only you can do."

In another setting, I would have guessed it to be an offer of sex, and I would have turned it down. I would not subject another to the horror that is my body. This conversation, however, is not about sex. It is a promise of something greater.

She sits across from me at my desk. Her eyes are black and full of stars. "I think you know why I am here," she says, clicking her tongue.

I pray that I do. I pray that she is here to whisk me away to a place where there are others like me, to tell me that I have been alone by mistake.

Instead, she says, "I am here to tell you that all of your medicinal needs can be solved with a little pill called Galataea." I collapse back into my chair, disappointed. I thought she knew me.

"Whatever your miracle pill does," I snarl, "we are not in the market for it."

The woman frowns. "I thought you would understand," she replies. "I thought you knew you were destined for something beyond this earth. It is no matter. Some are not yet ready." She stands up and offers me her hand. I take it, and as my fingers brush against hers, my vision changes from a drab office to images of the stars sparkling throughout the sky and galaxies swirling in the deep emptiness of space. I retract my hand with more force than I intended. "You saw it," she says, smiling to herself. "I knew you were better than this. I knew you were like me." I quickly usher her out the door.

Every time I close my eyes, I am transported back to those empyrean visions. I watch suns explode into fiery supernovas, burning quickly and brightly before crumbling to dust. I see black holes pulling entire planets full of civilizations beyond humanity's wildest dreams into its ever-expanding maw. I feel something I have never felt before. I feel at home.

I am kicking myself for my stupidity. I should not have let her go. I should not have been afraid. I race through the office and hurtle down several flights of stairs, faster than I have ever run before, praying that I might catch her before she is gone. On the sidewalk, I search frantically for the woman and the promise of a better life. I do not find either.

At night, I punish myself by looking at my body in the reflection of my windows. I am naked, once again picturing myself being taken apart and put back together, but this time, I am replacing my hair with the rings of Saturn and my arms with the arms of the Milky Way. My eyes are no longer blue or gray but burning white with the heat of a thousand stars. I pick myself apart, replacing each terrestrial organ with something celestial until I am not human anymore, and, for the first time, I imagine a picture of myself that I do not despise with every fiber of my mortal flesh.

When I open my eyes, I am human again, looking at my wretched reflection in the window. As my eyes adjust, I catch a glimpse of the outside. She is there. The woman from earlier. I dash through my house to the front door and burst into the evening air. "You came back for me," I whisper.

"Of course. I could not leave you behind." She extends her hand, and I take it once again. The images of heavenly bodies fill my mind anew.

"What are you?" I ask. "What am I?"

The woman pulls me close to her, and I open my eyes. "We are not from here," she says. "We are something else entirely. You have been lost for a long time." I stare into her eyes. She is correct. I was lost, but now I feel like I am home. She brings her face close to mine, and I meet her lips. As our skin touches, I feel myself tear apart. I do not fear it. Stars circle around us as I feel my body, no, this body that is not mine, lift off the ground. "Are you ready to go home?" she asks, no longer sounding human. Her voice is a euphony of light, like stars crashing into each other.

I cannot bring myself to answer. This body is no longer. I will never hear this human voice again. Instead, I can only sing the music of the spheres.

With all due credit to Kafka, etc.

THERESA JEAN TANENBAUM

One day I woke up and the skin of the woman
I'd been becoming
had sloughed off me
It stuck to the bedsheets starting to dissolve

I thought I knew what I was transitioning into
when I started HRT
but I didn't | couldn't | wouldn't
The *me* underneath my woman skin was
exquisite | resplendent | glistening
My sheets slimed with my rapidly vitrifying husk

A spreading puddle
Liposuction-pink
So femme!

It hurt much less than you'd think
until I realized my new dimensions would be
much harder to dress

"Am I going to need ANOTHER new wardrobe?
That's just unfair!"
Especially since I'd finally
found a style that felt like *me*
I should've waited, clearly,
'til I was done cooking

Theresa Jean Tanenbaum

The first time your body reshapes itself is
interminable | impossible | miraculous
You snap a selfie every morning and line them up
searching for any sign that it's happening
Is your soul kindled anew behind your eyes
or is the lighting just better this time?

My re-rebirth is more dramatic
Swift in its inevitability
The eyes that I'm looking at now
in the hand mirror from my bedside "dilation station"
are certainly burning brightly
Whorls of willo'wisp glow swirling around irises.

With preternatural grace I half-stand, half-leap
out of bed. Leftover bits
of that old meatsuit drip
and splatter wetly on hardwood

Face-unlock doesn't know me
and my fingerprints were left behind, stuck to the quilt
so I unlock my phone using the swipe pattern
Selfies are self-care. I can't resist snapping one.
What have I become?
I am breathtaking. I am monstrous.
I am everything I've always known.
Everything I was ashamed of admitting for so long

How can I explain that the parts of me
that seemed soft before masked jagged edges?
The people who knew me best
had all cut themselves on them like a rite of passage
or an intimacy test

Now that sharpness surfaces
The softness is still there
but so much harder to find
beneath new chitinous armor

With all due credit to Kafka, etc.

It will be hard to go out in the world like this
but my first three months of social transition
taught me more about public discomfort
than any cis person could imagine
It's a shame my old skin
is so gooey
Too tattered to slip back into
Too much a mask to feel like me any more

I spend an Entirely Appropriate amount of time
preening in the mirror on the vanity
admiring my new anatomy
as it refracts the morning light
slanting through the window

Am I :
    animal | or vegetable | or mineral?
    D) All of the above.

I don't even miss my woman skin. Not any more
than the man mask before
her, nor do I regret those years
spent hiding amongst humans

My therapist once opined that our lives have seasons
she was right about mine
I feel this new season of vengeance settle upon me
seep into the cracks in me, fan the coals
in my belly to a roaring ice cold
flame

I am not the only one, I know.
Awareness of awakening sisters grows
Each one exquisite and resplendent
Each one unique and unearthly
My girlfriends ping my phone with glee
A feed of sexy monster selfies

Theresa Jean Tanenbaum

"Did you get fangs?"
"I have seven tails!"
"Bitches, I've got a mane!"

I go to make a video
of my best attempt to blow
a kiss to the camera and that's when I discover
that the cold flames burning within me
can be exhaled
Breathe in through the nose
blow out through the mouth
The curtains catch fast
then the bed | the room | the house

I am birthed in flames, then,
tempered and hardened

Trailing smoke I take to the skies
while beneath me
the old me
dies

My will to be as I should, outweighs my will to live
Still, I shush the beast
Cause once again
I remember
This is only my
reflection

You Are Already Well

JEF ROUNER

Humble, Hoxsey
Tue, April 23 at 1:07 AM
From: <revhox@humblewatersofhealing.com>
To: Rene T. <p0pcornrene01@gmail.com>

YOUR WELLNESS JOURNEY STARTS NOW!

Greetings and blessings, Rene!

My team and I here at Humble Waters of Healing are so glad that you have joined our community of wellness experts and health truth seekers. In doing so, you have already taken the first step into a life free of cancer, pain, toxins, and corruption of the body and soul.

I see that you have signed up for the basic package, which includes a monthly shipment of our patented Miracle Water Solution (MWS), as well as daily prayers said by myself on your behalf. You will be charged $184.99 on the first of every month to the card ending in 1927. Please make sure that there is enough money in the account to cover the charge.

We draw MWS directly from our artisanal wells in the Grey Forest of Essex County Massachusetts, a place long revered by the Pawn-Truck-It Indians for its remarkable spiritual and physical healing properties. Cancer was virtually unknown among the Pawn-Truck-It Indians before the white man brought processed foods and vaccination to the land, which many scientific minds now attribute to the pure waters of the forest. We believe that proper application of MWS can teach the body to heal itself of virtually any cancer or illness.

While we know that $184.99 can be a difficult monthly expense, we feel it is well worth the cost for recovering people from the scourge of cancer (and far cheaper than Big Pharma!). Please consider upgrading your subscription to the gold tier ($309.99), which includes a state-of-the-art alkalinization of the water to boost its ability to align the body's energies for maximum wellness. We recommend this product particularly for people in your demographic.

Cancer is a menace, and you don't have to fight it alone, Rene. You are a child of God, and He wants you to be in full health. Please let us know when you want to upgrade. Your first shipment should arrive in 2-5 business days by USPS.

You are already well,

Rev. Hoxsey J. Humble, CCH
CEO, Humble Waters of Healing

Me
Tue, April 23 at 1:35 AM
From: Rene T <p0pcornrene01@gmail.com>
To: Humble, Hoxsey <revhox@humblewatersofhealing.com>

Re: YOUR WELLNESS JOURNEY STARTS NOW!

Dear Rev. Humble,

Thank you for your kind words! I have to admit I am terrified. Who wouldn't be if they found a mysterious hard lump on their chest and had no health insurance? I've always been very healthy (eating right and exercising every day) so it's inconceivable to me that I could ever develop cancer. Hell, I ran a 5k just last month.

Hopefully MWS will clear it up. I found the testimonials on the website very moving. Knowing that others have fought this and won brings me so much peace. I can finally go to sleep tonight free from worry.

As you said, I am already well! What a wonderful message! I can't thank you enough for your help.

Yours in hope,

Rene Trost

Humble Waters of Healing
Sat, April 27 at 11:35 AM
From: <noreply@humblewatersofhealing.com>
To: Rene T. <p0pcornrene01@gmail.com>

YOUR MIRACLE WATER SOLUTION HAS BEEN DELIVERED!

Dear Rene,

According to our online tracking system, your order of one (1) case of basic-level Miracle Water Solution (MWS) has been delivered! Please follow the instructions for application carefully.

Sincerely,

The Humble Waters of Healing Team

Note: this email address is not monitored, and replies will not be read.

BASIC MIRACLE WATER SOLUTION

Contains 31 8oz bottles of Basic Miracle Water Solution (MWS)

Instructions: Drink one (1) bottle of Basic Miracle Water Solution (MWS) every day. If desired, water may be administered via enema (enema kit not included).

Ingredients:
Distilled water (non-alkalized), sodium chlorite, citric acid**, magnesium stearate, artificial flavoring

Miracle Water Solution (MWS) has been extensively evaluated in many scientific studies and shown to destroy various harmful viruses, bacteria, and toxins, some of which are comorbid with cancer.*

*These statements have not been evaluated by the U.S. Food and Drug Administration.TheseAdministration. These statements are not intended to diagnose, treat, cure, or prevent any illness.

**activator

Me
Sat, April 27 at 4:25 PMM
From: Rene T <p0pcornrene01@gmail.com>
To: Humble, Hoxsey <revhox@humblewatersofhealing.com>

Re: Re: YOUR WELLNESS JOURNEY STARTS NOW!

Dear Rev. Humble,

Just wanted to drop you a line and tell you that my first case of MWS was delivered today! I was so excited to start the treatment that I chugged the first bottle without stopping. I swear I can already feel the MWS coursing through my veins. It burned a bit going down, but I can only assume that's the toxic die-off effect that I've read about online.

The lump on my chest seems smaller even just an hour after first administration. You truly are a miracle worker. I can't wait to tell everyone I know about your company. Is there a discount for referrals (ha ha!)? Because I plan to send you a lot of people.

Yours in blessed healing,

Rene

Humble, Hoxsey
Sat, April 27 at 8:56 PM
From: <revhox@humblewatersofhealing.com>
To: Rene T. <p0pcornrene01@gmail.com>

Re: Re: Re: YOUR WELLNESS JOURNEY STARTS NOW!

Dearest and most blessed Rene,

Thank you for your note and your kind words. Knowing the good MWS and God can bring in people's lives gives me so much joy. If I didn't have to pay my staff of researchers and bottlers, I would honestly hand out MWS for free. Sadly, man's world is still too cruel for that, so no, we do not offer referral discounts at this time.

You are already well,

Rev. Hoxsey J. Humble, CCH
CEO, Humble Waters of Healing

Me
Sunday, April 28 at 9:34 AM
From: Rene T <p0pcornrene01@gmail.com>
To: Humble, Hoxsey <revhox@humblewatersofhealing.com>

Re: Re: Re: Re: YOUR WELLNESS JOURNEY STARTS NOW!

Hey Rev. Humble,

I'm sorry to keep blowing up your inbox, especially on a Sunday when I'm sure you're preaching. I just have a quick question about MWS.

I've been keeping mine in the fridge because the instructions didn't say I couldn't. Who doesn't love a cold bottle of water? Anyway, I came down to my kitchen this morning, and I noticed that there was a glow seeping out from the edges of the fridge door. Must be a busted sensor for the light or something, right?

No, it was the MWS. I even took a bottle into the bathroom and turned off all the lights. The water is glowing a really weird color. I wish I could describe it, but all I can really say is that it's not red, not purple, and not green.

Even weirder, when I put the bottle up to my ear, I swear I can hear something. It's like TV static, but cyclical like waves. The noise is very faint, but it's there.

Is this normal? The water tasted the same. The burning was a little worse today. I assume all the toxic stuff in me is fighting back, but we'll beat them! Chest lump is the same size, but softer. That seems like progress!

Sorry again to bother you,

Rene

Humble, Hoxsey
Wed, May 1 at 10:48 PM
From: <revhox@humblewatersofhealing.com>
To: Rene T. <p0pcornrene01@gmail.com>

Re: Re: Re: Re: Re: YOUR WELLNESS JOURNEY STARTS NOW!

Rene,

Please forgive the lateness of my reply. I wanted to thoroughly investigate your question as we have the highest standards here at Humble Waters of Healing.

The slight burning sensation and changes to your cancer are to be expected. Praise be to God! However, the glow you are referring to and the noise you are hearing are not something that I have encountered before in MWS. It could be a mental side effect of the MWS, though you may want to see a doctor about possible visual and auditory hallucinations.

I would be careful about telling a physician about using MWS, though. Big Pharma puts great pressure on doctors to downplay the benefits of MWS in order to line their pocketbooks. It has led to harassment and persecution of providers like me, so for the safety of my family, consider your use of MWS a secret.

You are already well,

Rev. Hoxsey J. Humble, CCH
CEO, Humble Waters of Healing

Humble, Hoxsey
Wed, May 1 at 11:07 PM
From: <revhox@humblewatersofhealing.com>
To: Ammi P. <anpierce654@protonmail.com>

Fwd; Re: Re: Re: Re: Re: YOUR WELLNESS JOURNEY STARTS NOW!

Ammi, what do you make of this? Glowing water! This son of a bitch is crazy, right?

Click to see forwarded message.

Pierce, Ammi
Wed, May 1 at 11:23 PM
From: Ammi P. <anpierce654@protonmail.com>
To: <revhox@humblewatersofhealing.com>

Re: Fwd; Re: Re: Re: Re: Re: YOUR WELLNESS JOURNEY STARTS NOW!

Shit, with all those waste treatment plants upstream around Lawrence and the runoff from that drug-testing kit lab, I'm surprised the water doesn't fucking bite people. Granted, the well on my great-granddad's land should be safe from all that. It's up in the blasted heath, and I'm pretty sure the groundwater doesn't mix with that city trash.

The last trip for well water was around Easter. Usually, I try to make sure the older barrels are in front so that we're at least sending fresh water, but my nephew is lazy and may have just put the new barrels out in the mixing bay. Even if he didn't, MWS is like a quarter bleach. Hard to imagine anything harmful surviving in it.

I'll head out to the storage facility in a day or two and tell you if I see anything glowing lol.

Click to see forwarded message.

Humble, Hoxsey
Thu, May 2 at 12:09 AM
From: <revhox@humblewatersofhealing.com>
To: Ammi P. <anpierce654@protonmail.com>

Re: Re: Fwd; Re: Re: Re: Re: Re: YOUR WELLNESS JOURNEY STARTS NOW!

Thanks, Ammi. It's bad enough having the FDA chasing us. Don't want to add the EPA to the list! In all likelihood, this customer is just nuts. G'night.

Click to see forwarded message.

Me
Thu, May 2 at 8:33 AM
From: Rene T. <p0pcornrene01@gmail.com>
To: Humble, Hoxsey <revhox@humblewatersofhealing.com>

Re: Re: Re: Re: Re: Re: YOUR WELLNESS JOURNEY STARTS NOW!

Rev. Humble,

I think something is wrong. My stomach hurts really bad. I went to the bathroom today, and something big and pink fell out. I had to fish it from the toilet so it wouldn't clog. It wasn't, forgive me, poop. It was still pulsing. And glowing.

I was hoping maybe it was the tumor, but the lump on my chest is still there, and now it's bigger. I drank two bottles yesterday. Is that why this is happening? Please advise.

Rene

Humble, Hoxsey
Thu, May 2 at 11:11 AM
From: <revhox@humblewatersofhealing.com>
To: Rene T. <p0pcornrene01@gmail.com>
Re: Re: Re: Re: Re: Re: Re: YOUR WELLNESS JOURNEY STARTS NOW!

Rene,

Passing infected flesh does sometimes happen with MWS. I am gathering my scientific team to investigate your query. Please stand by and cease application of MWS for the time being.

You are already well,

Rev. Hoxsey J. Humble, CCH
CEO, Humble Waters of Healing

Me
Fri, May 3 at 4:33 AM
From: Rene T. <p0pcornrene01@gmail.com>
To: Humble, Hoxsey <revhox@humblewatersofhealing.com>

Re: Re: Re: Re: Re: Re: Re: Re: YOUR WELLNESS JOURNEY STARTS NOW!

Glorious Rev. Humble,

The good news: the glowing is out of my refrigerator.

The better news: *IT'S INSIDE ME NOW, REVEREND!*

You are truly a miracle worker. After my last email to you, I was so thirsty. I've never been thirsty like that before. Regular water wouldn't quench it. Soda did nothing. Neither did milk or juice. My head was pounding. It was like a heartbeat in my skull, but not a human heart. The beating came in five bursts. BA-dum-dum-BA-dum. Does anything have a five-chambered heart?

I know I shouldn't have drank all the MWS at once. You said to follow the instructions, and I pride myself on being a good listener. It's why I was so angry at the lump. I did everything I was supposed to! Never smoked, never did drugs or drank. Me getting cancer was a cosmic mistake. I just needed something to correct it, and the lump would fade.

It seems silly now, wanting the lump to fade. That lump is huge now, and beautiful. It's like a porthole into me. The skin is translucent, and the glow is everywhere. My entire world is not red, not purple, and not green. I turn off the lights and lie naked in the dark, watching the colors and shapes inside me swirl and dance on the ceiling.

When I run my hands up and down over my body, my fingers sink into the flesh like dangling my hand in the water from a rowboat. It feels nice. I am pliable and throbbing, filled with God's light. Everything else is fading away. Last night I passed a pile of bones and organs in the toilet. It didn't even hurt.

Please send me another case as promptly as possible. I've placed a new order for the gold tier, but I wanted to give you a heads up so it wouldn't get flagged as a double order mistake. Enjoy the picture (attached) I took of my lump! You have my permission to use it as a testimonial on the website.

Glowing,

Rene Trost.

Humble, Hoxsey
Fri, May 3 at 9:01 AM
From: Ammi P. <anpierce654@protonmail.com>
To: <revhox@humblewatersofhealing.com>

Fwd: Re: Re: Re: Re: Re: Re: Re: Re: YOUR WELLNESS JOURNEY STARTS NOW!

Ammi, I need you to get back to me ASAP. Did you see the picture this guy sent me!? Human bodies aren't supposed to look like that.

I swear to Christ I am buying you a cellphone after this!

Click to see forwarded message.

Pierce, Ammi
Fri, May 3 at 9:16 AM
From: Ammi P. <anpierce654@protonmail.com>
To: <revhox@humblewatersofhealing.com>

Re: Re: Fwd: Re: Re: Re: Re: Re: Re: Re: Re: YOUR WELLNESS JOURNEY STARTS NOW!

Hox,

I just got back from the mixing bay, and I think we're fucked.

Sure enough, my lazy nephew put all the newest barrels in front, and all of them are definitely glowing. It was so bright it nearly blinded me when I walked in, and that noise . . . yeah. Your guy was right. It's like listening to an hourglass full of ants all scrambling not to fall through.

I don't get it! We've been pulling water out of that well for nearly a decade, and the worst thing that's ever been in it was a dead bird. This is some insane shit.

My grandpa used to tell me a story that some weird meteor came down on a nearby hill when he was little. Said that's why all the trees were grey up there. The meteor did something to the land.

Always thought it was a bigger pile of bullshit than this bleach water grift, but now I wonder. Maybe radiation?

Whatever it is, you're right. Human bodies aren't supposed to look like that. What do you want me to do?

Ammi

Click to see forwarded message.

Humble, Hoxsey
Fri, May 3 at 9:25 AM
From: Ammi P. <anpierce654@protonmail.com>
To: <revhox@humblewatersofhealing.com>

Re: Re: Re: Fwd: Re: Re: Re: Re: Re: Re: Re: Re: YOUR WELLNESS JOURNEY STARTS NOW!

I'm driving up there now. Be there in half an hour. You'd better be home and make sure that idiot nephew of yours is there, too.

Click to see forwarded message.

Pierce, Ammi
Fri, May 3 at 9:31 AM
From: Ammi P. <anpierce654@protonmail.com>
To: <revhox@humblewatersofhealing.com>

Re: Re: Re: Re: Fwd: Re: Re: Re: Re: Re: Re: Re: Re: YOUR WELLNESS JOURNEY STARTS NOW!

I told you from the beginning this whole thing was going to get us in trouble! Conning sick people out of their money with well water and bleach. Jesus. My mom died of cancer. I can't believe I let you talk me into this.

Click to see forwarded message.

Humble, Hoxsey
Fri, May 3 at 9:44 AM
From: Ammi P. <anpierce654@protonmail.com>
To: <revhox@humblewatersofhealing.com>

Re: Re: Re: Re: Re: Fwd: Re: Re: Re: Re: Re: Re: Re: Re: YOUR WELLNESS JOURNEY STARTS NOW!

You were singing a different tune when you bought that F-350! Goddamn you and your stupid nephew and your whole stupid clan of fucking hillbillies. I am amazed you could mess this up.

Be there when I get there, or I swear to God I will burn your house down.

Click to see forwarded message.

Pierce, Ammi
Fri, May 3 at 9:50 AM
From: Ammi P. <anpierce654@protonmail.com>
To: <revhox@humblewatersofhealing.com>,
<p0pcornrene01@gmail.com>

Re: Re: Re: Re: Re: Re: Fwd: Re: Re: Re: Re: Re: Re: Re: Re: YOUR WELLNESS JOURNEY STARTS NOW!

Go fuck yourself

Click to see forwarded message.

Humble, Hoxsey
Fri, May 3 at 9:52 AM
From: Ammi P. <anpierce654@protonmail.com>
To: <revhox@humblewatersofhealing.com>

Re: Re: Re: Re: Re: Re: Re: Fwd: Re: Re: Re: Re: Re: Re: Re: Re: YOUR WELLNESS JOURNEY STARTS NOW!

DID YOU JUST HIT REPLY ALL!?

Click to see forwarded message.

Me
Fri, May 3 at 10:08 AM
From: Rene T. <p0pcornrene01@gmail.com>
To: Humble, Hoxsey <revhox@humblewatersofhealing.com>, Ammi P anpierce654@protonmail.com

Re: Re: Re: Re: Re: Re: Re: Re: Fwd: Re: Re: Re: Re: Re: Re: Re: Re: YOUR WELLNESS JOURNEY STARTS NOW!

Oh Rev. Humble and Mr. Pierce,

Please don't worry on my account. I don't even mind that you are criminals. Did Jesus not personally promise a thief a place in Heaven? Why should I be less merciful than he?

The lump is so much larger now. I had to carry it in my arms when I left the house. I thought it was strange the way it almost looked human, like I had just gotten married and was bringing my bride over the threshold.

When I stepped outside, I took a great big breath. I mean, really really big. I must have breathed in for half an hour, my new lungs filling with air and expanding my glowing lump into enormous size. It rose like a balloon up above me, glowing its wondrous glow and bathing me again in its light.

You Are Already Well

I was a bit frightened when my feet lifted off the ground. Heights scared me, even as a kid. That was when I was breakable, though. This time, the fear passed as the lump pulled me skyward, its winged tendrils waving in the air as I dangled vestigially from it by my chest.

I've tried to take a picture of the lump for you, but I'm afraid the angle is just not going to work. I was lucky enough to see it reflected in the glass of a skyscraper as I passed through Dallas, though.

Beautiful. I am so beautiful now. The lump has grown into a massive head at least four times as big as my body (how lucky I am to be there as a point of reference). I think it's a human head, though I can't be sure. Light flashes from the eyes and mouth and nostrils.

Will it keep being born from me, do you think? I've birthed a winged, giant head! Will shoulders and arms come next? A torso and legs? Will I become the lump on ITS chest, then? Or maybe I'll curl up and be absorbed to become its heart, beating and throbbing and, for now, typing on this little phone while the battery lasts.

That's what I would like.

People will probably be scared. I saw screaming faces in the skyscraper windows. I wanted to tell them to be not afraid, but then I started laughing and spinning around. My twisty skin is so fun to play with.

From here I watch the world go by, holy and healed. I am drifting toward Massachusetts, where I can see the glow you sent me in your bottles. Wait for me, dearest Rev. Humble and beloved Mr. Pierce. See the miracle you made.

I am already well,

Rene Trost

Click to see forwarded message.

TRIANGLE SIMULACRUM

ESTHER ALTER

ONE

A fucked up centaur thing with tentacles and a beard pries open your door slaps its feet into your house slams you to the floor holds you down looks around the room wide eyes swiveling separately finds a pen uncaps it brings it down to your shoulder presses too hard this is when you scream you can feel a trickle of blood.

And then it's over.

All the centaur's eyes look at you. From those eyes down to what passes for its torso, it's all teeth and esophaguses. The torso is long lines of muscular tissue merging and branching out again: vertices, lines, and just air in between.

The centaur stares at you a tentacle slaps your face another one presses your skin where the pen was, and the pain is a lot. You try wriggling away and the centaur lets you and you curl up into a ball and you assess the damage. On your shoulder the word "ACCEPT" has been written in precise, crisp lines that have been smudged by seeping blood.

Your boyfriend is screaming and then there's a loud wet crunch and he has stopped screaming.

You look up. The centaur's long neck is wrapped around your boyfriend's body and it's gnawing on his body and blood is leaking out of his body. You consider saying something and then you remember the word on your shoulder so you just watch.

The centaur finishes off everything above the neck line moves one of its gross feet over you and you have an overwhelming sense that a question has been asked that requires a yes/no answer.

"No" doesn't feel like it's in the spirit of the bleeding word on your shoulder, so you say: "Yes."

And that's when the centaur presses its foot into your stomach and fills you up with triangles.

***

TWO TWO

***

You are in pain while the triangles shred your insides and turn you into a polygonal obscenity a foreign object a beauty seeker a scorpion deployment system a perfect blade an extraterran infiltration asset a tougher faster stronger very very very angry woman.

***

THREE THREE THREE

***

When you catch up with the centaur, it's already made it to the facility.

Behind you is a path of natural complexity resolved into geometric purity. Humans, houses, military ordnance, all have become triangles. As you passed them, n-hedral tires slipped on and fused into perfectly smooth road surfaces, crashed into each other, severing limbs off of triangulated drivers. One car hit a fire hydrant and spears of water exploded outward, are still exploding outward. You were shot at, but your scorpions shielded you.

Brave soldiers of the Army of the United States of America await you at the facility. With a flick of your wrists, small triangles fly out of what was once your skin. When they impact real-world subatomic particles, they decompress into sharp-edged scorpion-like entities that clatter on hundreds of legs toward the soldiers. The soldiers aim and fire but your scorpions leap upwards and intercept the bullets. The remaining scorpions reach their targets and slice them apart.

Then it's just you and the centaur.

It chews on a soldier-corpse while waiting for you to make the first move.

You scream and throw triangle-scorpions but the centaur deploys squares that block and break your scorpions and you bellow with rage because every scorpion destruction costs you something akin to agony.

The centaur's squares are destroyed microseconds later by the antiquadrilateral field surrounding the facility. Oh yes, the United States of America knows about this fucked up centaur, has known about it for a long time, and knows that the centaur wants the thing stored in this facility. But the United States of America doesn't know about you, or your triangles.

The centaur stares at you coolly shifts its stance articulates its tentacles to imply something disgusting about your dead boyfriend. So you deploy your scorpions again, but this time they scuttle past the centaur and unpack into two dimensions and slip through the walls of the facility.

You can't see the beauty contained therein but the data returned by your scorpions makes you gasp gasp gasp in adoration. The centaur transformed you such that you would infiltrate the facility and fall in love love love with this perfect thing and devote the remainder of your existence to its protection. You want to kiss kiss kiss it. It is like a mother a lover a confidant a political allegiance a puppy a dyke a song a mountain a thunderclap a stillness a drop of pond water, a miracle a miracle a miracle that you can just barely perceive. But then you perceive something else, a flaw a bug an emotion coursing through your geometry-logic: crude unassailable human spite.

Your scorpions puncture desecrate eviscerate that beautiful holy perfect thing.

The centaur realizes what you're doing falls to the ground writhes excretes something like tears from its eyes. The tears contain pheromones that communicate that it would be mutually beneficial if you were to show mercy. You cry too, extruding tear-shrapnel that perforates your eye sockets.

You have broken a fundamental covenant with the concept of beauty. You will grieve for a thousand thousand thousand years. But it was worth it because you got to make that ugly fucked up fucked up FUCKED UP centaur feel like a total piece of shit.

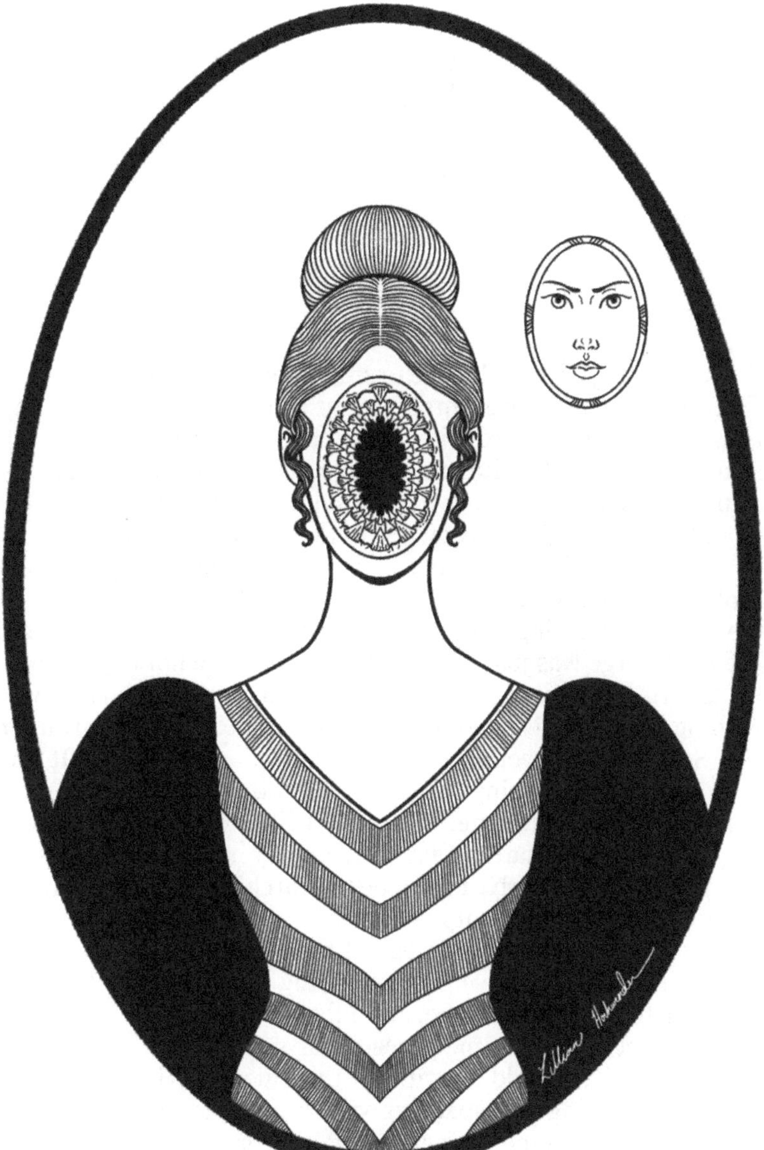

Please

Lauren Coffin

Personally, I would like to stop handling things well.

Like last week, for example: when Uncle George gathered up his nerve to have a word with me at the family cookout. Eyes all hard and full of self-righteous courage. Angry little mouth. Sort of asking and sort of ordering me, he said, "You're telling someone about the static?" Even my sweet mother shook her head.

Look. I snatched the paper plate from his hand and Frisbee'd it into my cousin's rusty above-ground pool. It felt incredible. Saw one of the kids fishing wet burger buns out as the aunts circled me, told me George was just an ass like that, told me not to goad him on, escorted me to my car so he could have time to cool down. Nothing came of it. No apologies and no further words from either side. So what good would composure have done me, then? It was an ugly and embarrassing thing to do. I get that; it was also honest, which has stuck with me. I think I'd like to stop acting right altogether. Unfortunately, that is an awfully hard habit to break.

Ever since the party, I have been searching for any feeling of regret. All I've come up with is a craving for dumpling soup.Something about the image of the burger buns in the pool. Well, today's the day. I've got everything but the garlic. I'll get a nice walk to the grocery store, and I'll get my fill of salt and carbs, and I will get ahold of some peace for myself.

Admittedly, I could do without the blue sky. The static pops against it, dancing and sparking vividly, hard to ignore. But the cool air wakes up something giggly in me. I breathe it in as deep as my lungs go.

Please

State law says I was supposed to report myself weeks back. They set up their database and brought in those federal agents; a matter of national security, etc. I preferred it when they used to say we were all just suffering from mass hysteria. If Uncle George rats me out, maybe that'll be my line: *sorry, officer, the man on the TV told me I was crazy, and I believed him. I must have missed the episode where he told me I was dangerous.*

Everything I'm a danger to right now resides solely in the Stop 'n Shop snack aisle. I'll need some fuel while I cook. The walk signal lights up across the street, and its afterimage burns into my vision, a paradoxically bright shadow. Almost holographic. The static likes to hold onto shapes. I blink extra, which doesn't help, and look around, also not a solution. But a good distraction. Somebody's got their corgi wearing a blue ball cap. I bet their cookouts are a delight.

My walk does me such good, I'm singing under my breath as I near the grocery carts lined up by the door. I hang back to let a guy wrangle his grocery bags out of his cart. My eyes land on the bland white entryway walls, the perfect background for the static to storm and rage against.

"You okay?"

Another woman is standing nearby, watching me, ash growing long on the lit cigarette in her hand. She must have seen me staring too intently at the wall. She asks, "What's it like?"

I think about what my worst reaction to this question could be (maybe putting her cigarette out on her sweater?), but then it strikes me what she's asking.

Not the usual, the repetitive, the incessant, *what does it say?* She isn't asking about the message buried in the static. She's asking about me. What is it like to be me right now?

"It's . . . intense," I answer, leaving too quickly after. But I slow down a little when I come back around with a cart, and I add, "Please know, it's also kind of beautiful."

I head for the snacks, wondering at myself. A fascinating choice of words back there. Beautiful, I said. I guess there is something to that; only a sliver of the population can see the message, and as poorly transmitted and vague as it may be, it still represents a key moment in human history. First contact and all that.

Another shopper rams into my cart.

I pull back and wave them on with a quiet, "Please, go ahead." That right there. Exactly what I'm talking about. I am trying to carry a fire in me, but I keep smothering it out with self-control. Come to think of it, if I can't help doing this, it must be the very opposite of self-control.

I fill my cart with a distinct lack of moderation in mind. On the way to the produce section, an employee offers me sample cheeses, and I think to try out over-exuberance. I say, "Oh, yes, please!" It feels off. Forced, even. The fluorescent lights in here have gotten the static all stirred up, like it's frantic. Time I get my garlic and go home.

I scan the produce shelves, whispering, "Please don't be out," with an odd sense of foreboding. The message in the static has taken on an unusual clarity. It's pushing to the foreground like fingers digging through dirt, pale and flashing, and it is, it really is beautiful. Nonetheless, I am still trying to find the garlic.

The message is a hundred different words simultaneously. Other receivers translate it to something like *see*, like *stop* or *don't*, like *understand*. But more than anything, I always thought it was like . . .

"Please," I say out loud. Mist sprays over the leafy vegetables, coalescing here and there in droplets. The word is like a droplet on my tongue, cold and wet and gathering more of itself.

"Please," I say again, my hands touching my throat.

The word has been crawling around in my mouth all day. How many times have I said it without noticing? I try again, but:

"Please?"

Nothing else will come out now. "Please." I'm not just seeing the message; I'm hearing it, tasting, touching, "Please." I think I'm starting to become the message.

"Please," I say again, louder, more insistent.

I'm becoming one word.

"Please," I yell.

If I keep repeating this word that I'm becoming, if I say myself so many times it no longer makes sense, what will I be?

"PLEASE," I scream, pressing my palms against my eyes in a hopeless attempt to block the static out. When I remove my hands, I still see static, and I see people staring at me, too. That's when I remember that it's beautiful.

Please

All of them. And me, and the word, and most of all, the scene that I am causing- so beautiful it aches.

I scream myself again. Not asking anything. Telling everyone. Answering the question of all of us, what we were, who we are, how we always will be.

P

Please

L

E

Please

A

S

E

The garlic is just on the other side of a nearby display. My lips bleed from stretching. Catching my breath, I take two bulbs and drop them in my cart, finally. Silence everywhere. Even the music has stopped playing overhead.

I ready myself again, my word, to be louder, and louder, and louder still with a tremendous inhale.

Silence (Screaming)

FAYE HOPPER

On the day the world ended Hannah tried to fuck and failed (I hate you I hope you die).

She had been trying to fuck for a while. She was really horny. More than that, she wanted to be touched. Touch made her feel alive, and most of the time she felt like a corpse and her loved ones (there are fewer of them by the day) were just temporizing on the burial because they didn't have the money.

She got on Grindr for the first time in years. A hot-seeming tgirl (the image never tells the truth because the image is staged and truth can only be observed in absence of self-conscious poses) hit her up.

She was in town for a work trip. She was staying in one of those ritzy hotels that's more-or-less a skyscraper, right in the city center. Hannah took the elevator to the very top floor and went all the way to the back.

The girl (her name was Faye just like me) was sitting on the bed. A pistol lay on the duvet between her spread legs. Her pale face and chestnut ringlets and purple eyes were very pretty.

"I want to die. Will you help me kill myself?" she asked.

Hannah mulled it over.

"I won't. Sorry. Why do you want to die?"

"I mean, isn't it obvious?"

"I mean, yeah. It's tough. I'm sure you've been through a lot. We all have. That's no reason to end it all."

"I'm tired. Everything's too much right now. No one loves me. Everyone hates me."

"I doubt that's true."

"How would you know? You don't know me."

"Yeah. I guess I don't."

And then there was silence.

"Would it be okay if we put the gun to the side? You're really pretty. Can I kiss you?"

She mulled it over (please touch me).

She started to cry.

"Yeah. Okay."

She put the gun on the nightstand. Hannah sat on the bed next to her. Hannah wrapped her arms around her (me). She kept crying (I remember when they screamed at me after I hit myself because they wouldn't stop being mean I remember when those kids laughed in my face for the crime of walking on the sidewalk I remember how she still called me big boy when I was inside her even though she knew how much I loved dresses and the new name I remember how the eyes of everyone at the DMV bored holes in my back I remember every atom of every moment the knives ran cold on my skin please make it stop).

"Poor baby. It's really tough, huh?"

Hannah notched her fingers on her chin. She tilted her head up. The kiss was so soft. It staunched the tears.

Hannah shook. She was hard (I was hard too; grieving and sex are similar).

And then something slit the sky like a yonic cut (as it is in painting because no real laceration is that neat and semiotically charged). And then a withered hand reached out to crush the sun. And then emaciated legs stretched from the hole and commenced a creaky cavort and the skyscrapers (we screamed when the rocks of the roof came crashing down I don't want to die) were rubble under the bony feet and the sea swelled at its steps to drown the ones who weren't, by then, a smeared and scarlet stain on the shattered sidewalk. And then the long and lank body emerged and stretched from pole to pole and the atmosphere popped like a balloon and the Earth broke apart when the twiggy legs dug like drills in a spray of dirt and detritus all the way from the topsoil to the molten core at the heart to the cold vacuum where hoarfrost shrouded its toes. And then its shriveled lips gobbled up the most delectable bits with cupidity and it flicked flecks from its matted beard and the sated glint of black eyes in the black of space was centuries later a glimmer in some cyan sky with three suns [one red for hate one blue for love (or was it the reverse) one purple for what happens when the two fuck and have kids] where four-eyed magenta children with suction cups where we'd have hands and a language of chitters sounding from the stridulations of their chitinous limbs (it made sense to them and no one else just like us) capered in appreciation and spent many moments of their millennia-long lives wondering what the miracle could mean. And then where the Earth once was there was nothing. And then the old thing smiled and licked its lips and its stomach gurgled and it danced through the Universe until it too was pulled apart. And then, when everything was gone, it ate itself.

And then there was silence (I love you please don't go).

We Are the Devil in the Body and Mind of a Young Woman

Bitter Karella

They call it "the female," when they call it anything at all, and it sometimes speaks in riddles that, when deciphered, are said to predict the shape of things to come. But mostly it speaks blasphemies and gibberish, and the older priests, who are well versed in such things, can only get it to cooperate by dousing it in holy water and commanding it in the name of Jesus to speak truthfully. Once, a young priest eager to make an impression with the Monsignor, attempted to pour sacramental wine down its gullet, but it snapped off two of his fingers and he did not try a second time.

The priest who guards the door of its chamber is of the old school and clearly prefers these methods to the pioneering, cutting-edge ideas advanced by Father Redacted, for he usually only greets Father Redacted with a scowl and a grunt when the latter comes to speak with it. But today the old priest says, in a not unkind voice, "You shouldn't speak to it so much. It'll get in your head."

"I don't let it in," says Father Redacted. It is cold and damp so far under the earth and Father Redacted shivers in his cassock.

The old priest shakes his head. He is stoop-shouldered, with long greasy gray hair and rheumy eyes. His teeth are yellow and his fingers tobacco-stained, although Father Redacted has never seen him with a cigarette in all his years on the Fifteenth Sublevel. Father Redacted does not smoke, but he longs to feel the same sensation of burning vapor in his lungs, if only as a ward against the chill that permeates everything down here.

"Everyone thinks that," says the old priest as he unlocks the door for Father Redacted. "Until they do."

***

We are the devil in the body and mind of a young woman. We have occupied this vessel for some time, long enough that we can no longer sharply recall the start of our tenancy. Perhaps we have always been here, but it was only in recent years that our host has finally been able to hear our whispers. Or perhaps she could hear us the whole time and it is only of late that she has begun to pay us heed. In any event, there is no longer a *me* or a *her*. There is only us. We are one, united in purpose and in strength.

Let us describe ourselves. For a long while, the woman had faith in her heart and she entreated the Lord for a mercy that the Lord, in his wisdom, refused to grant. In her folly, she turned to false gods and invited us in. There is nothing else to say about that. We are a mighty and terrible king of Hell, with two hundred legions of demons under our rule. We understand all the languages of man and we can give dreams to those we favor. We can teach all arts, philosophies, and sciences, and we know the location of hidden treasures below the earth. A conjurer must face northwest, the direction of our house, when they seek to summon us. We appear as a fine man of handsome countenance, wearing a golden crown, and our body is covered in shining black scales like a fish. We possess a fine virile member and a bifurcated tail, and, below that tail, in the place where you would have an anus, we have a second face. We are splendid. Any man should be so lucky as to gaze upon us.

Let us describe the room in which we now live. It is cold and windowless, decorated with seals and sigils and circles over which the law has forbidden us to pass, and it is deep in the basement of a very large building the location of which we do not know. There is a mattress on the floor and the walls are padded. All day, we listen to the moaning from beyond, sometimes quiet, sometimes loud, rising and falling like a distant lullaby, so many voices muffled almost to a whisper by the padded walls. We have a King James Bible, which is linked via a hook in its spine to a chain connected to a ring in the wall. We avoid that. In the far corner of the room, there is a lingering stench around the yawning mouth of an open pipe. This is where we must shit and piss. On the floor, there is a large black circle circumscribed with a pentacle and surrounded by even more arcane sigils. These accoutrements impede the power of demons, though humans can pass through them without obstacle. The priests instruct us, through a hatch in the door, to stand at the center of the circle, and only when they are satisfied that we are thus contained do they dare to enter the cell with us.

Our care is entrusted to a rotating series of priests, so we can guess that we are below a cathedral or possibly a basilica. We can sense the distant throb of holy objects above, like the opening strains of a migraine headache. The priests come with food, which we eat voraciously, and with Holy Communion, which we spit upon the floor with howls and shrieks. We are naked, because the priests fear we would hide the chewed-up wafers among our garments and use them to affect escape; for the same reason, they inspect our crevices daily. The priests regard us with amused contempt, taking liberties to run their hairy hands over our chest and jab their fat fingers into our taint, but they jump back when we snap at them. Despite everything, they fear us. That fear makes them hate us all the more and that hate makes their inspections all the rougher. They torment us until we cry out and they jab their fingers deeper until we scream.

One day, a new priest comes to see us. His hair is gray and his forehead is creased from excessive worrying. He sits upon the floor across from us and speaks to us. We scream and flail as is our way, but he remains calm. He asks different questions than the other priests.

"Would you like to take communion?" he asks. None of the other priests have ever asked us that. We hiss and snarl, because the body of Christ would destroy us.

"If you could take communion, you know you could leave this place?" says Father Redacted.

"If we take communion, we will leave this place," we say, and he believes that we are confirming his statement rather than speaking a prophesy of the future. "The other priests don't say things like that."

"The other priests are set in their ways."

"But you're different? What's the point of taking communion? You think salvation is possible for us?"

Father Redacted closes his eyes, a remarkable display of foolish trust. "Before I joined the seminary, I went to school to study the workings of the human mind, and I learned that it is possible for the mind to become convinced of nearly anything. Healthy people can convince themselves that they are sick. Strong men can convince themselves that they are weak. And a woman can convince herself that she is the devil."

This priest is kind. He does not touch us, nor do the other priests touch us when they are in his presence. But he sometimes sees the bruises on our legs, the lashes on our stomach and he says nothing. So we know his kindness comes from weakness, and we hope to use that to our advantage when the time is right.

***

Let us describe Father Redacted. He lives in a small cell on another level of this basement; he has a bed and a little chest of drawers, where he keeps personal items, including a photograph of his mother, who is surely dead by now. In his youth, his heart was aflame with the glory of God. But now he is older and he is subject to all the doubts and worries that maturity brings. He has not ventured to the surface in many years, because his work here requires constant attention, although sometimes, at night, he dreams of a faraway village on some distant shore, where the sun peeks through the coconut trees and turns the evening sky a beautiful velvety purple, and there is a man there. Father Redacted does not tell us these things, so he believes that we do not know them.

"I don't let it in," he reminds himself before he goes to sleep. Then he thinks of the scars on our body and he feels a deep shame. He thinks of us shivering in our cold cell and he feels a great pity, and yet he still thinks he has not let us in.

***

"If you could just eat the wafer, I could help you," says Father Redacted. "That would be enough to prove to them all. I could tell them I saw you do it. Maybe I could convince them to let you go? They would, I know they would. The Monsignor is a reasonable man. I wish I could help you. That's why I joined the priesthood, to help people. Please, let me help you." His eyes fall upon the silvery scars that slash across our belly, that split our breasts like canyons.

"Why would you want to help us?"

Father Redacted is quiet.

"We are a sight to behold, if you could see us as we really are. We really are quite wonderful. We have beautiful black scales that glisten in the light. Never did our scales shine so brightly as when they reflect the flames of Hell! We have fine strong powerful wings like a great bat, vast and leathered, and a virile member like a horse, thick and long but with smooth, velvet skin. Every inch of us is too glorious for you to comprehend."

Father Redacted is embarrassed by such talk; he is a priest, after all. "I'll speak with the Monsignor," he says, his cheeks pink. "I'll at least make sure they don't hurt you again."

***

There is another fact which we know about Father Redacted: Sometimes, when he does not dream of the village on the beach, he dreams of us. We have the power to torment him thus. We claw at his cassock, fumbling with the buttons and ripping the cloth, until we peel him from his vestments and regard him, up and down, like a cat inspecting a cornered rodent. We flick our little pink tongue across our lips.

He thinks he has not invited us in

We hook our fingers into his mouth, and he feels the point of our talons bite into his cheek until he drools blood. The heat of our body against him is intense, like a burning furnace, and as we move he can feel the hard thorny knobs of our scars brush his skin. Our scales are bathed in the glow of hellfire, shimmering and iridescent, like liquid obsidian. It would be a beautiful sight to see, because we are radiant to behold in our native land. He can feel tongues of flame lashing his body, singeing his skin until it blisters and bubbles, under the permanent sunset orange of a flaming sky, and it is so deliciously warm. He would do anything to bask in that warmth.

Our breath is like an abattoir. Father Redacted smells of old cigarettes.

***

It is sometime later that we meet the Monsignor for the first time. He is a tall man, very thin, like a skeleton. He has a sharp nose like the beak of an eagle and rheumy eyes that drip constantly. He is very old and wrinkled and, unlike the other priests, his black robe is trimmed in red and has a red sash. He does not touch us, but he commands the lesser priests to injure us on his behalf while he sits on a small folding chair, his finger to his temple, and watches. The lesser priests are especially enthusiastic in their work while he is watching, so we must assume that the Monsignor is a man of high rank well worth impressing.

***

"Who did this?"

The priests have injured this body many times, but never before have they been so thorough. It is broken, possibly irreparably so. Its condition must be grim indeed, because we can hear Father Redacted crying.

We are able to reply because the tongue is among the few parts to still work: "Many priests, working together, under the orders of the Monsignor."

"The Monsignor? No, no, that couldn't be. It couldn't be."

Father Redacted starts to blubber and bawl, and make noises of impotent masculine fury.

"I'm trying to help you," he says when he regains the power of speech. "Don't you understand? If you could take the communion, you could leave. If you could just eat the wafer, then I could do something!"

We shriek and flail. He waits for us to complete our tantrum and then he says, in a quiet voice, as if he is afraid that the walls have ears, that the old priest outside the door might be straining to hear: "I want to take you out of here."

"Then take us," we say.

Father Redacted fidgets. He claims to be a rational man, but for all his study of the mind he cannot shake the superstitions of his youth, not even now when the furnace of his faith has gone out. "Show me that you're no devil. Show me you're cured." He holds the wafer up for us to see. "If not for yourself, then for me. Don't you think it hurts me to watch you like this? Don't you think it tears me apart?"

Eating that wafer will kill us, we have never been so sure of anything.

"For you," we say and we open our mouth. He is always letting us in.

Father Redacted places the wafer delicately upon our tongue.

It burns. It is the worst pain that we have ever experienced in our entire existence. We close our mouth.

Father Redacted is a fool. Doubt has grown in his heart. He is used to tormenting helpless children and, deep down in his heart of hearts, he has allowed himself to think that we are simply one more such wretch.

"Do you know what this means?" Father Redacted leaps to his feet in excitement, his face beaming. We have never seen him so overjoyed. "It's just like I said! There's no devil in you! By the love of God, there's no devil in you!"

Our body is in pieces, and we can feel the communion wafer melting the flesh beneath our tongue. The pain is excruciating. Father Redacted is smiling, clapping his hands in childish glee. He is filled with the exuberance of a man who has not been happy for a very, very long time and who had all but forgotten the taste of the feeling—like a drowning man tasting air. He crosses the threshold without fear, the delightful fool, so brimming with joy that he could just melt our heart, and scoops our body into his arms. He smells like old tobacco.

It is a great relief when Father Redacted removes us from this place, past the reach of sigils and circles and signs, and it is with some satisfaction, because it has all been orchestrated so perfectly, that we are able to show him our scales and he can agree that they do indeed shimmer so splendidly.

Contingency Protocols

WREN HEARN

[You hear the fat, churchy chord of a pipe organ the size of Creation, making you feel melancholy with a ragged edge of annoyance. The sound shepherds down for a few moments and rolls off as an immense, weary sigh.]

ˋˏ-ঌ UGH ৎ-ˎˊ

ˋˏ-ঌ Here I am, enjoying the Super Fun Math Orgasm dimension, where cumming is like breathing—and I am a LITERAL ANGEL—sucking and fucking my way through the heavenly hosts as an abstract geometric paradox—when some black stars appear in the firmament and bathe all the lands in darkness and despair and I just know this is some whack Carcosa nonsense. You ignorant simps. You can't even do "mystic cult" right. Why not just let the Heavens be? You just had to fuck shit up. ৎ-ˎˊ

ˋˏ-ঌ Okay, well, fine. Let's do this. ৎ-ˎˊ

ˋˏ-ঌ I've been around forever. As long as you have, or longer. You can't even comprehend that. This is how unworthy you are. I know all the tricks, so like, right after the black stars there's these headlines like: "The Yellow Sign—Is it Really a Path to Madness?" and "Time—Flat Circle or Bumpy Rhombus? We Ask Diner Patrons in Hastur Their Thoughts." And why the fuck exactly did we need an Independent Review of Angel Identity Services for Children and Young People anyway?! I cannot possibly roll my ophanim farther back into my abstract geometric immaterial head—because I know what's coming.

I'm going to have to take care of this and doing that means giving up my wings and the constant sacred math orgasm of this higher realm and abandoning immateriality itself . . .

. . . for the physical realm where I am merely an entire planet. I'm a really bitchin' one, too, with purple rings and four-hundred moons hanging colorful as jewels in the wine-dark sky. The oceans are pink with flowers, great feminine swirls of them. I look so good, you wish you were me. There're people here, too. Well, some variety of person thing that you probably are inventing slurs for as we speak.

They worship me, their planet. We get along great and I take care of them. Well, mostly they take care of each other. I just visit each one to check in and make sure they have everything they need to thrive. OMG you should read the reviews I get. Really sweet. "Xenohospitable," they say. There's a queue to make landfall on me. Of course, I don't make them do that (queue up), they just think there's scarcity where none exists. I can grow and refine myself to care for all (you! can! too!). All are welcome. Well, not you Carcosa freaks. I dunno why your community is full of weirdos and sucks and mine is full of hot alien sluts and rules but maybe you should think about that.

My onboarding process is very thorough. It lays out the luxury communism amenities and all the various ways of familying together (and not) in the kith-not-kin family-abolished beloved community. It's rad. We actually don't have any weapons here lol. If you don't count the books. So while I'm wrathful (nonpracticing) I'm fuelling myself with joy for the fights ahead. Me and my flock enjoyed this state of things for a geologic age.

But then you wormy shits made a superweapon and fired it at me. (Some notes: your power-up sequence is washed, and woww another be-greebled Platonic solid the size of a moon, how original!). I had to scramble to sublime my surface inhabitants—

yes, including all the little critters :3—into Angeltown where my friends could look after them for me while I fight you sloppy sad sacks. So now that my mantle is shattered (thanks btw) I escape myself in the planet's core, which is actually a huge . . . ☆

⁂ . . . Continent-class Omni Systems Vehicle (also pink) now zipping along an asymptotic curve through your hostile volumes at 5,684c, 31 million puppygirls hanging their tongues out the window in the cosmic breeze. ⁂

⁂ Yeah, there were other people living in the core the whole time. They do the whole hedonist utopia thing: glanding drugs, recreational sex changes, modifications to become more animal- or alien-like, sacred raves and disco sacraments, and tons of sex. They barely need me. I just clean the litterboxes, really. ⁂

⁂ Cramming my consciousness into this tiny compute substrate (tucked discreetly into mountain range on my terraformed half) is already uncomfortable but I've spent my rest wisely, preparing myself for the long war. Oooh, a computer! You're calling me a computer (manish)! "This thing could never be alive, much less a biological woman!" I don't really know how to convince you of this because the computers you make suck shit and have too many fingers—but a being of exotic matter with the mass of a moon and a copy of every video game ever made can definitely be a woman. Maybe it sucks shit to have body standards at all? ⁂

⁂ Anyway, I have weapons now. You're sending fighters, a dense swarm eating my gridfire and pulsed maser and anti-matter scatter. Well, congrats, that's a lot of fighters. I can't shoot down that many. Who keeps funding you? This is what I wonder as I eject my inhabitants in variously-sized escape vessels, safe and comfortable, into the void. Not all of them. A few hacked the controls (I didn't make it hard—some need to fight) and did some incredible cowgirl shit and blew a hole in the primary weapon of the Boring Platonic Solid (erotophobic) but not before it had a chance to fire again so I'm being wrent from my colossal ship body into . . . ⁂

A clipper. A screaming fast destroyer. I'm a heavily customized, hot-rodded tugboat the size of a city melted against the grid pushing 1312↑c. Just me: no passengers, no crew. I'm so fast and sleek (and pink) I can't be seen by your eyes. They're too slow. Slow eyes, how embarrassing.

I give merry chase, behind your lines, hitting hard when I can. I last a while. Six seasons and a movie. Eventually, you encircle me by converting a few percent of the mass of the universe into war machines, gender cops, and grey tabloids. It wasn't even thrilling. Perfunctory legal maze-building.

Where is all this coming from? Oh? Some moldy gargoyle who lives in a castle and likes sorting, instrumentalizing, and torturing kids? Well, understandable. Perfectly understandable. You simply had no choice but to align yourself with cisness, and then nationalism, and fascism, and so on. As I'm forced into retreat after retreat, diminishment upon diminishment, you're so sore at winning and this hate so core to your being that—

Ah, fuck. That one was abrupt. Almost put me on the list of names.

We learned the lessons of epistemicide early. Our militant archivists established aggressive backup procedures. We don't just build a library. We put legs on it, jumpjets, and guns. We install another escape contingency, too. We make it eighteen stories tall. Like the Elasmotherium FK12 Mech Chassis now making planetfall above the North Sea, ablative drop cocoon peeling away in layers from a dense core gouging a scar into the highlands and vaporizing Loch Tay. Oh, it's me! That's me, I'm a mech now. (pink)

My ferrous-carbon and molten red steel behemoth begins to lumber into Aberfeldy, strobing lasers searching for targets among the barely recognizable ruins of a castle. Even with ground-penetrating maser composite imagery, the castle has ground itself into the earth so completely it's hard to tell. I stop there, pondering, alert. Bristling for an ambush.

४⁀➴ I feel the yearning, for my friend-lover-comrades who have their own backs against the wall and feel isolated. Final girls from the moment we birthed ourselves. I think of you and harden myself. ४⁀➴

४⁀➴ No attack comes. At least not from here. Only the ones I brought with me, a few minutes behind. Of course the hag (derogatory) that flicked the domino has been long dead and you're just the endstate of this relentless seeking out of every bit of difference to yoke and stratify. You're all miserable as a result. You can't attack me without subjecting yourselves to the same differential. Your sacred dies cut even the compliant shapes. ४⁀➴

४⁀➴ Yawn. Eepy Carcosa. ४⁀➴

४⁀➴ Well, come at me bro. I fire my magazines dry and eject as the heat from powerful IR columnation melts the mech from around my plug. The plug shoots skyward and deposits me in a neatly punched hole in the side of your superweapon. I tumble into . . . ४⁀➴

(੩˙ᗜ˙) . . . My new body! You know, those things you think determine your destiny? One of those, but like what a cool person would imagine. Pink (in some places at least). Fur. Do I have a dick? I know you're wondering, because you weirdos are obsessed with policing peoples' junk instead of trying to liberate The People's Junk. You're going to be so happy though. I have like 5 dicks now. Some are big, some are small, one does a loop, and they all have incredible mouthfeel. A few pussies, too, at least two buttholes I know of, and a lot of other stuff we thought up with pleasure militants in Angeltown. But, ya know, all demurely tucked. (੩˙ᗜ˙)

(੩˙ᗜ˙) So, how's it going bestie? im in ur suprwpn fuckn wit yer doods. I have crystal swords and knife missiles and I'm good with voices so things are getting pretty Bugs Bunny up in here. I'd prefer, like, y'all to just chill out and let yourself and others get their freak on. You'd be much happier! I mean it, so serious. Blood is really hard to clean and my fit is only partially hydrophobic. (Sorry about that hallway.) (੩˙ᗜ˙)

(ʒ˥˙ᴗ˙) “Wow, what a monster,” you’re probably saying. “Sufficiently violent and brutal in attempts at its own liberation to justify any oppression.” Anyway. I’m glanding delta-9 progesterone and CHEMICAL X and getting my razorgirl on. Wetware radiating ectogenesiac tactical wombs. My young living in your walls. All yr code is pwnt beyond recognition, but who could even tell? ¯_(ツ)_/¯. I’m cloaked in voidsilk barely a whisper of smoke in the visual spectrum, chopping audio of your unguarded moments to play back to you tauntingly. Credit where due that’s a cute sneeze (mine now) but you didn’t need a nose anyway. You’re just going to have to irradiate the entire Solid, which you’re doing with the rest of the fleet, still arriving (finding parking). So I’m incandescently irradiated with an impressive assortment of charged particles and am shunted into . . . (ʒ˥˙ᴗ˙)

⌬ . . . Well, if we weren’t monsters before, we’re skittering little freaks now. The xecofeminist weapons labs have been cooking. Tentacles (some are also dick tentacles, but in an octopus way) and feet (snail) and claw (mantis) and mandibles (yautja) and ears (sled dog) and tail (wagging). Well, kill to kill, it’s something different. Always something different. That’s what you hate. ⌬

⌬ We’ve communized the means of survival (yet again) in that our protomolecules have cracked the biological properties of exotic matter to use this bombardment of radiation as metabolic fuel so instead of a mummified hot dog, microwaved too long, our body goes Fat Akira instead, cracks open the Solid like an egg and expands to fill a substantial volume of the (cisness hegemonized) universe. There’s an anomalous membrane, beyond which a vast siphonophorous fungal disco blooms. The last ecotone. You doomed fools, you’re sending expeditions into the heart of us. You have to listen to us, as we drive you mad, about everything and how you’re fractally wrong, even as our hostile ecology smears your expressed genome across your face like pie before letting our medusoids and zooids feast. To a hyperpop beat. Pay it no mind. ⌬

⌬ There's just no escaping it. Our queerness is going to bloom within you. In your children, if they hide well enough from you. In those you love. We have friends everywhere. ⌬

⌬ Each defeat makes us more weapon. Each victory makes us softer. We are not beings of scarcity where weaponness makes us less soft, or our softness makes us less weapon. ⌬

⌬ You have a nice armada. No, really. It's fine. Establishing a perimeter. Digging in. Measuring our glacial expansion. Getting anxious. You don't know it yet, but we're in your holobiont. We're sideloaded viral DNA, recombining and latent within your precious, hygienic gene pool. I told you, we've been here forever. We have shit in all your bathrooms. There will never be a time we have not always been. Your expeditions haven't even made it to the card catalog much less the occult section. Yes, we are the library. We make the Culture. Your books are in here, too. You weren't so big on libraries since you were the papers, the publishers, the chyron in control of what or who is pulped. We've read them and, well, bless your hearts. ⌬

⌬ [Sotto voce] Please, for the sake of the patrons, shut the fuck up forever. ⌬

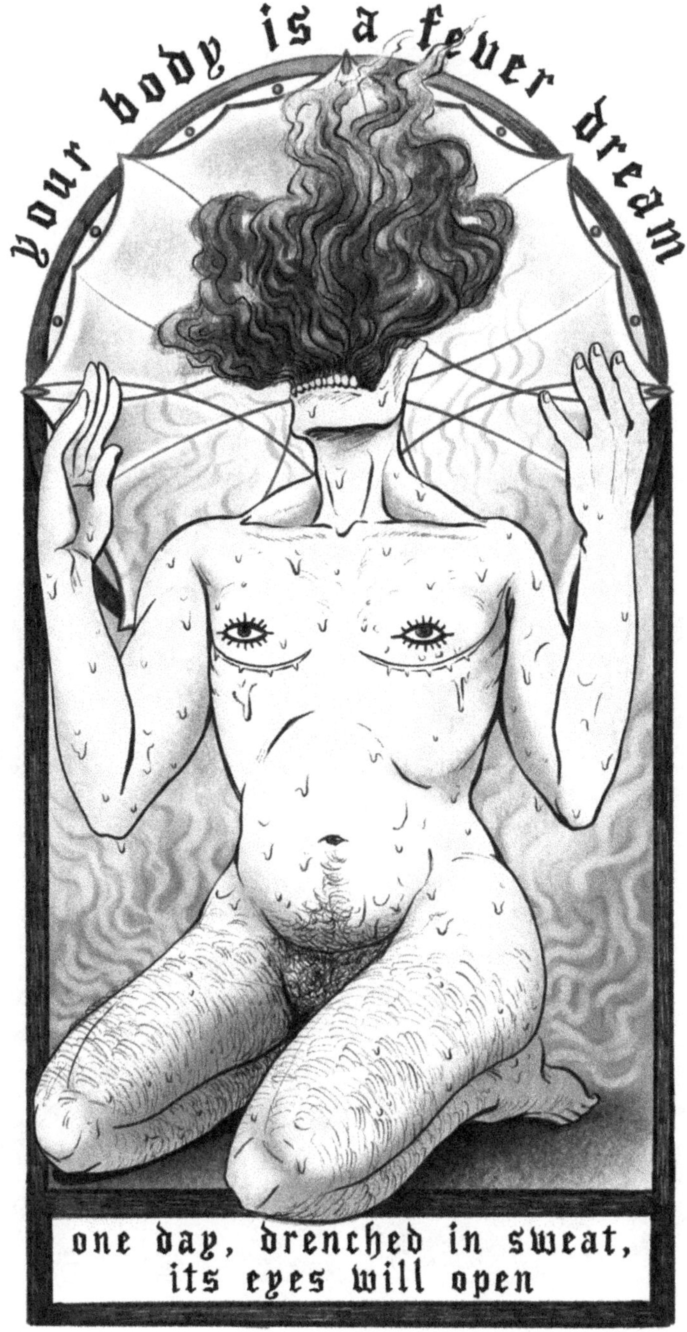
your body is a fever dream
one day, drenched in sweat,
its eyes will open

About the Contributors

Acantholichen × variifolius (they/them) is a nonbinary Singaporean Peranakan in Naarm, Australia. A speculative biology enthusiast, they exclusively write monsters, reflecting the rich complexity of human experiences: weaving in gender exploration, chronic pain and the wonders of witnessing nature. They apologise to real biologists and zoologists for any inaccuracies for the sake of fantasy and cool creature design.

Alex Hera is a writer, film director, and alternate reality game developer. At a young age, Alex was exposed to weird independent horror projects on the internet, and they were never the same.

Alex Woodroe (she/her) is a Romanian writer of dark speculative fiction and Shirley Jackson Award-nominated editor-in-chief of **Tenebrous Press**. She's the author of *Whisperwood, The Night Ship*, and *Tatratea*, and has several short stories and articles published in venues such as *Nightmare Magazine* and the Nosleep podcast. Alex lives in the heart of the Transylvanian region of Romania.

Ariel Marken Jack haunts a crooked house in Atlantic Canada with three black cats, three small harps, and one enchanting spouse. Their writing has appeared in *Canthius, Fictionable, Fusion Fragment, Heartlines Spec, PseudoPod, Strange Horizons, The Year's Best Canadian Fantasy & Science Fiction*, and more. Work and words at arielmarkenjack.com.

Ashe Thurman is a writer and ex-indie game developer out of Texas that would volunteer as host for a symbiotic alien intelligence maybe a little too quickly. Their other work and occasional nerd rant can be found at pixelsandpins.com.

Avi Burton (they/he) writes strange, sad, and speculative fiction. One of their first stories was published in the original *Your Body Is Not Your Body* anthology, and they are thrilled to work with **Tenebrous Press** once again. You can find more of Avi's work on their website, www.aviburton.com, or on Bluesky, @aviburton.bsky.social.

Beverly Litkin is a San Francisco Bay Area writer and comic artist. She's a trans woman, athlete, activist, lefty futurist, and recovering alienated techie, living as bisexual and queer as possible. Her own sex change did nothing to diminish her interest in gender-bending stories, which she now seeks to elevate beyond their roots as a permission structure for repressed transfems.

Bitter Karella (He/She/They) is a genderfluid transvestite goblin and creator of the three-time Hugo-nominated microfiction comedy account Midnight Pals. Her novella "The Ballad of Horse Girl" was published by **Tenebrous Press** in *Split Scream* Vol. Five, and his first novel, *Moonflow*, is now available from Orbit. Their second novel, *Quaint Folk*, is scheduled for publication in October 2027.

Chris! is a giant ageless creature trapped in a human body. Known as "smoll Dad" around Little Ghosts books, he serves as creative director and (f)art department for the bookstore x press. Most likely spotted fawning over toll Dad and his dog, Bruce.

Dave V. Riser is a genre-hopping ghoul. His work has appeared in a number of other places, including The Arkansas International, *Bloodletter Magazine*, and *Dark Matter Presents: The Off-Season*. Find him on Bluesky @davevriser.

Elena Sichrovksy (she/they/it) is a queer disabled author and cult survivor. They find gender euphoria in deep sea creatures, Don Hertzfeldt films, and the soundtrack from *Annihilation*. Read more of her published poetry and prose at elenasichrovsky.com.

Esther Alter is a trans Jewish writer, game designer, and open source software programmer. Her fiction and poetry can be found in *The Deadlands, Baffling Magazine, khōréō, Reckoning, Escape Pod, Strange Horizons*, and the anthology *Amplitudes: Stories of Queer and Trans Futurity*. She lives in Massachusetts. Follow her @esther-alter@bsky.social or check out her website esther-alter.com

Emilija Vavic is a poet from the Gulf Coast of Texas and a Design/Technology student at her local university. You can find her on bluesky and insta under @those-em-and-ems.

Faye Hopper (she/her) is a writer of fiction and poetry based in Philadelphia. Her work has previously been published in *Mixed Success Magazine*. She hopes to show people visions of other worlds.

Gabrielle Bleu writes luminous science fiction and fantasy. Their work has appeared *in Solstitia, Astral, Alien Fiction*, and in the *Gargantua anthology* by Air and Nothingness Press, among others. Find more of Bleu's work at gabriellebleu.com, or follow her @gabriellebleu.bsky.social.

Genesis enjoys long walks on the ocean floor and eating detritus. His exoskeleton is looking very vibrant this time of year.

Guoldu is an artist and game developer hiding out in the Pacific Northwest. In his spare time he is personal chef to 2 cats and 1 food-critic of a pitbull.

H. Marin (she/they) is a disabled queer author of dark speculative fiction, the novelette editor with *Foofaraw Press*, and a current MFA candidate at Fairfield University. Her work has appeared in *Night Shades Magazine* and is forthcoming in *If There's Anyone Left, Pulp Asylum,* and *Rat Bag Lit,* among others.

Helen Whistberry is the pen name for an indie author and artist. Their whimsical artwork often focuses on the natural world, and they enjoy creating original drawings to accompany and enhance their writing, which explores their own experiences with gender, asexuality, alienation, and autism. You can find out more by visiting their website at www.helenwhistberry.com.

Jackie Marley is a writer and researcher living in Brooklyn. Their work has appeared in *Stopgap, Phenomenal World*, and several academic journals. Originally from the British Midlands, they hold a PhD in philosophy.

Jef Rouner (they/them) is an award-winning journalist, host of the Friday Nightmare on TikTok, and horror author from Houston, Texas. Their work has appeared in *Dark Spores, Oklahoma Pagan*

Quartley, and the *Society of Misfit Stories*. Two collections of their stories, *Stranger Words* and *The Rook Circle*, are available from CHBB Publishing.

Jordan Kurella is a trans and disabled author who has lived all over the world (including Moscow and Manhattan). His work has been nominated for the Nebula Award, the Sturgeon Award, and the LA Times Book Prize. He has three books published.

K. Brown (they/them) lives in the Southeast with their partner and cat and too many plants, painting, drawing, writing and doing weird things with linux and wireless technology. They are slowly putting together a website for all of this at http://unknown.garden. They've been trying to find the entrance to Midian since 1992.

KJ Martinet is a non-binary comic artist and printmaker making work about identity, existential loneliness, and interpersonal relationships, usually using risograph and silkscreen.

Lillian Hochwender is a writer and visual artist whose work often explores mortality, marginalised identity, and the Gothic. Their past work includes indie album covers, an illustration in **Tenebrous Press**' *Your Body is Not Your Body* anthology, and a collaboration with the disability charity AbleGamers. They have a soft spot for 19th century literature and can usually be found under a cat.

Lyd Low is a queer Asian-American artist based in the Midwest. Despite their nyctophobia, they find comfort in romancing the macabre through their illustrations, stories and songs.

Mariah Southworth is a horror and science fiction writer and illustrator from the Pacific Northwest. She likes her fiction like she likes her reality: queer coded and too weird to be believable.

Maxim Volk (they/he) is a queer speculative fiction author from the Midwest. Their work has appeared in *Acorns, Carnage House, The Palisades Review*, and more, and their first book *Deadbeat* is available from Slashic Horror Press. You can find them on Instagram @maximvolk1.

Mx Morgan is an artist and illustrator based in the Pacific Northwest. Their work is best known for its use of macabre themes, animals, and nature, communicating our innate relationship to the natural world and emotional connection utilizing animals and mythical beasts. When not making art, you can find Morgan nerding over dinosaurs, biology and nature, playing too many games, or cuddling their black cat.

Morgan Wodring (he/they/it) is a neuroqueer pagan living in York, UK with Dorset roots. A molecular biologist by day, it spends the remaining hours painting, weaving and writing.

Ri Stypula is a writer of weird, queer horror who once almost became a mortician. Their short work as appeared in *Ghoulish Tales* and *God's Cruel Joke,* and their debut novella *Squelch!* is published by Merigold Independent. They have a BA in English from Seton Hill University and live in Greensburg PA with their partners.

Theresa Jean Tanenbaum ("Tess") is a queer, polyamorous, neurodivergent, disabled, transgender woman, and a witch. She writes and produces music under the name of Moth Mother, creates weird single-player RPGs, writes cozy queer romance novels and speculative poetry, and brews her own homemade black walnut ink. In a previous life she was a tenured professor at a major research university but now she lives in the woods with her wife, four cats, bearded dragon, seven chickens, five ducks, and her increasingly feral son.

Wren Hern's work has been published in *Project 2052: Revolutionary Dispatches from the World of Everything for Everyone* (Common Notions). She can be reached if you are pure of heart.

Xeni Flowers is an illustrator based in the Pacific Northwest. Their work uses surrealist body horror to describe aspects of identity, disability, and mental illness.

Xosh M. Belanger (he/him) is a Shirley Jackson, Stoker, and British Fantasy Award nominee, two-time recipient of the Joseph Cotter Memorial Poetry Prize, and author of several dozen books, including the *Dictionary of Demons* and the *Shadowside Series*. Intersex, introverted, and feral, Belanger resides in NE Ohio and can often be found gaming under a pile of cats.

Yomi Torrens is a non-binary digital artist and an aspiring indie comic creator whose artwork tends to be a mixture of cute, creepy, and whimsical pieces.

Ziggy Schutz (she/him/he/her) is a bigender, disabled butch who is at all times looking for ways to make his favourite fairytales and horror stories reflect people who look a little more like her. You can find more about his writing at linktr.ee/ziggyschutz.

The following pieces were originally published elsewhere:

"All Her Rows of Teeth" originally appeared in *Three-Lobed Burning Eye*, Issue 42, July 2024.

"Light Amidst The Plains" was originally published as a *Dose of Dread* by Dread Stone Press (R.I.P.)

"She Calls Me Love" originally appeared in *If I Let You Eat Me*. Self-published. 2025.

"What Spectrum Unfurls" originally appeared in Books by Marcel: *All Myths Are Trans*.

"With all due credit to Kafka, etc." originally appeared in the self-published book *Abominations: Poems of Feminine Monstrosity, Transformation, and Horror*. 2026.

CONTENT WARNINGS

Being a work of mature Horror, a degree of violence, gore, sex and/or death is to be expected. Many of these stories are centered around Body Horror specifically.

Additional notes have been provided below at the individual authors' requests:

"I Am Become A Cathedral" contains body dysmorphia, depression, alienation, agoraphobia, and general mental health breakdown.

"You Are Already Well" contains medical grifting.

"TRANS-ASCENDANT" features scenes of medical trauma.

"Songs for Solar-Powered Cowboys" contains mentions of surgery and parasitic infection.

"Silence (Screaming)" contains suicide, self-harm, and transphobia.

"Pareidolia Content" contains psychotic break, hallucinations, and reference to queerphobia.

"Pin Feathers" contains sexual assault, femicide, and religious abuse.

"In Space No One Can Hear You Cum" contains sexual assault (off page).

"Devotional for the Starved" contains cannibalism.

"Feast of Saints" contains self-harm, cannibalism, auto-cannibalism, auto-orchiectomy and religious imagery.

"Contingency Protocols" promises glorified fantasy violence against gender fascists.

"Hatred Enthrones Me" features depressive thought patterns including passive suicidal ideation.

"Tape Experience" contains scenes of addiction, body dysmorphia, and child death.

"what spectrum unfurls (beyond)" features misogynistic harassment.

Please be advised.

More information at
www.tenebrouspress.com

WEIRD TIMES DEMAND WEIRD READS:

ONE HAND TO HOLD, ONE HAND TO CARVE
M.Shaw

Two halves of a human cadaver awaken on a cold morgue slab, remembering nothing of their previous existence as a singular body. Their impending schism will lead them on separate and frightening paths forward.

A Weird, surreal Body Horror journey; Wonderland Award Winner for Best Novel, 2023.

"Bold, grotesque and oddly touching" - Andy Davidson

FROM THE BELLY
Emmett Nahil

A strange man is found alive within the belly of a whale. He is rescued and brought aboard the whaling ship, where a series of accidents, deaths and horrific transformations immediately begin sweeping through the crew.

Now they must contend with the vengeance of the sea made flesh, as well as the consequences of their own greed and destruction.

"A taut work of horror" - Publisher's Weekly

CASUAL
Koji A. Dae

In a dystopian near-future, Valya manages her anxiety with the help of her neural implant, CASUAL. But now she is pregnant, and the law forbids her from using CASUAL as sole caregiver to her unborn child. Her returned panic attacks have her considering a controversial clinical trial that would place a tandem device in her vulnerable child.

Casual is a stark and cutting glance at a near future that looks uncannily like our present.

"Up there with Atwood, Bradbury, Dick, and Gibson" - Literary Hub

PUPPET'S BANQUET
Valkyrie Loughcrewe

Married couple Celia and Martin are brutally attacked on their drive through the Irish countryside. The attack leaves Celia with a violent schism in her mind, seemingly existing in two places at once: one the "real" world, the other a howling, monstrous maelstrom.

Of her husband, there is no trace...until weeks later, when he is discovered in a bizarre hospital, his body spliced together with that of an unknown woman...and they are very pregnant.

"Not for the faint of heart, but its impact is undeniable." - Booklist

REEF MIND
Hazel Zorn

The coral reef rose from the seas, spreading across the land with incredible speed.
A rapidly evolving invasive species.
It transformed the landscape.
Mutated every living creature of the surface world.
We never suspected it had a plan.

"A new voice in Weird Horror worth keeping a close eye on." - Michael Wehunt